MEANS

Office Roulette, Book One

Kennedy Layne

MEANS

Dedication

Jeffrey—Business and pleasure do mix…and I wouldn't have it any other way!

Cole—Choose a profession that you love. Success *will* follow!

From USA Today Bestselling Author Kennedy Layne comes a sexy trilogy that involves greed, power, and the desire to do it all over again...

Smith Gallo has everything a man could ever want at the tip of his fingertips, except of course the woman he loves. To what lengths will he be willing to go to make his ambitions come true?

Laurel Calanthe is one successful stock pick away from making partner when she finds herself in desperate need of an alibi. There's only one problem. The man who can save her from being arrested is her only competitor and the one who now holds her fate in his hands.

Greed is a powerful motivator in the game of making money, but desire can overcome even the strongest motive.

CHAPTER ONE

" I COULDN'T BRING myself to end it."

Laurel Calanthe pulled open the pristine glass door that led to the offices of Manon Investments. The well-established hedge fund catered only to high net worth individuals and select business partnerships. The expensive décor was designed with those clients in mind.

In all honesty, even the air smelled of the same linen used in the manufacturing of U.S. currency. The heavy fragrance hanging in the air never failed to bring a smile to Laurel's lips.

The fact that the door was unlocked meant someone was still burning the midnight oil, but that wasn't unusual in their line of business. Brad Manon was fanatically selective in who he chose to add to the employment at his firm, most often ensuring the analysts understood loyalty and the importance of total commitment. Such marked dedication went the whole nine yards when it came to bonus time.

It was going on one o'clock in the morning on a Friday night, but that didn't matter in the financial world. One of the world's markets was always open, trading, and willing to take money from the fund's capital holdings.

"You've worked too hard to give up your success for Smith Gallo," Grace reprimanded, her voice of reason coming through loud and clear over the cell phone. Unfortunately, no advice she offered now could take back the fact that Laurel had just spent the last three glorious hours in Smith's bed. "I'm not saying that you shouldn't have a personal life, but does it have to be Smith? You're both up for partnership. How's it going to look if word gets out that the two of you are sleeping together?"

"That I've got tremendous taste?" Laurel asked halfheartedly, recognizing that she'd only put off the inevitable. It wasn't good for her career to get involved with her competition nor was it wise to dip one's quill in company ink. Oh, Smith had definitely dipped his quill in company ink. She'd even questioned if the partnership wasn't why Smith had propositioned her to begin with, though their attraction had started long before either of them were up for promotion. Did he believe he could ruin her chances if Brad discovered their indiscretions? "I know, I know. I'll tell him tomorrow that we should take things down a notch or two."

Soft backlighting accentuated the empty reception area, though she didn't pause on her way across the tiled entrance. She had one last destination in mind for the workday, and that was her private office where she'd left some files she'd planned to take home with her this weekend. Her black high heels clicked on the marble tile with each step she took until she reached the plush carpet of the private hallway.

"A notch or two?" Grace wasn't being fooled in the least. "I was at today's morning meeting, Laurel. The papers in your hand almost combusted from the way Smith was staring at you. Taking it down a notch isn't going to cut it, not even close."

"You only noticed that because you already know about the two of us."

Laurel continued to walk down the hallway, noticing that a dim light was coming from Brad's office. His private domain was located at the end of the corridor. The spacious corner office overlooked the beautiful city of Minneapolis, but he wasn't the type to have an open-door policy. Quite the opposite. It hadn't always been that way, but his demeanor had changed in the past few years…and not for the better.

It seemed it was in her favor to have stopped by for the files she needed, even at this time of the night when her boss was still here. Her presence in the office so late on a Friday would look good come next week when a final decision was to be made regarding the partnership slot.

Her chance at turning the fates was in the making.

"Look, Smith has a reputation for business and with women." Grace muffled a yawn, reminding Laurel of the time. "Mixing the two together is just a recipe for disaster. I don't want to see you get hurt."

Laurel rested her tongue against the back of her teeth in an effort to counter that sentiment. Smith only allowed the world to see what he wanted them to see, and nothing more. He'd been born into one of the most prestigious families in the city, but he'd worked hard to make a name for himself based on *his* contribution to society. He was an enigma to most of the people he interacted with on a daily basis. He was nothing like his spoiled siblings who lived off their trust funds while traipsing around the world with the jet set crowd.

"I'm not going to get hurt," Laurel argued, not truly believing her own contradiction. She had no idea where she stood with Smith, other than the sex was scorching hot. "Listen, I can't talk about this now."

She reached around the wall of her office and flipped on the overhead light. She hung the strap of her purse on the door handle before continuing down the corridor. Her heels sunk into the plush carpet as she got closer to Brad's office door. It would ultimately benefit her if she dropped by and checked in, letting him see that she took her work seriously.

"Brad's working late," Laurel said, lowering her voice so that it didn't carry through the empty hall. "I should say hello so that he knows I've been by."

Laurel waited for Grace to acknowledge her bid at goodbye, not bothering to stop outside the doorway. She took a step into Brad's office. The upcoming moment was mapped out in her head like a gambit in a game of chess.

She'd finish her phone conversation, not letting on that it was a personal call. He didn't need to know that she wasn't speaking with the London office. Such an appearance could only assist her in the meeting by the board in regard to the partnership, in which Brad's opinion weighed heavily with the other partners.

Unfortunately, her night just went from bad to worse.

"…got an early breakfast with my mom," Grace explained with disdain, not having the best relationship with her mother. Grace had no idea of the gravity of horror Laurel had just discovered. "Give me a call when—"

"I think…I think he's dead."

Laurel closed her eyes in disbelief, ignoring the hot sensation that practically singed her lashes. She hadn't been sleeping well lately, and with the amount of overtime she'd been putting in at the office and additional hours she shouldn't have spared in Smith's bed, it was obvious she was having an acute panic attack.

The grisly sight before her didn't change when she blinked her eyes multiple times. She tried to curtail her rapid breathing, afraid she would hyperventilate on one of the gasps in the back of her throat. She leaned back against the doorframe of her boss' office and did her best to stop retching. She attempted to recover, seeking the support of her best friend, along with a dose of realism.

"Grace, I think he's dead," Laurel managed to say once

again, her voice no louder than a whisper as she struggled to maintain what little composure she could muster.

Brad Manon couldn't be dead.

Things like this didn't happen in her life. That belief was what made her think that this was nothing more than a sick joke. That was plausible, right? After all, Brad used to pull pranks all the time, not that they were all that funny. She remembered when he'd feigned getting his fingers stuck in the large paper shredder in the copy room, causing Blair to spill her coffee all over the Xerox machine.

Of course, that had been back in the days when Brad had mingled with his employees, claiming he wanted low employee turnover and for his analysts and traders to know they meant something to the company. It was when this place was run like they were all family, and not the standard financial organization where everyone became cutthroat with one another trying to climb over the other's dead body.

"Who's dead?" Grace asked skeptically over the phone line in her usual calm demeanor. She wasn't the type to lose control over a situation. "And why are you whispering?"

"I think Brad's dead." Laurel pushed out those horrid words around her constricted throat and clenched stomach. She looked back over her shoulder toward the foyer, but no one came out of their offices laughing like they were pulling off some sick joke with Brad. "Come to the office now. I'm going to call 911."

"Brad? Our Brad?" Grace laughed in that soft angelic manner everyone had come to love here at Manon Investments. She was one of three employees who settled the trades implemented during market hours, quite content with her role at the company. "Are you sure Josh isn't hiding behind a door somewhere? He or Stan are probably catching this on video right this moment. You're so going viral by morning. You'd better get yourself together."

Laurel's gaze was still glued to Brad, whose body was currently leaning back in his chair with his head to one side. The gaping wound across his neck didn't look painted on or stuck to his skin, like one of those Halloween rubber embellishments. It cut impossibly deep.

This wasn't any kind of joke.

It was then that reality started to dawn on her that she might not be alone in the many offices that could provide a hiding spot for the guilty party. She didn't want to take a step even a millimeter closer to Brad, but she was afraid to walk back down the hallway for fear that someone would try to do the same thing to her as they had done to Brad.

"Grace, get your fucking ass here now," Laurel practically spat through her clenched teeth, doing her best to remain calm. "Brad's been murdered. He's dead, as in *dead* dead. I'm calling the police."

Laurel quickly disconnected the line, though her trembling fingers made it almost impossible to switch her cell phone's screen over to the dial pad. She succeeded after a few times, finally pressing the three important numbers that would bring help immediately.

Oh, my God.

Brad was dead.

"911, what is your emergency?"

"My boss is dead," Laurel blurted out, cringing when she took another tentative step forward. She didn't want to get too close to the body, but she didn't want to stand too close to the door, either. "He's been… He's been…"

Laurel couldn't bring herself to say aloud that Brad had been murdered or that his throat had been slit down to the bone. Her stomach began to revolt every time her gaze landed on the gruesome sight.

This can't be happening.

"Ma'am, what is your name?"

"L-Laurel Calanthe." She tried to breathe through her nose, but it was then that the scent of the coppery smelling blood became somewhat overwhelming. She briefly wondered if she was going to throw up the remains of her dinner. To quell the urge, she began talking and couldn't seem to stop. "My boss is dead. Literally. He's sitting at his desk with his throat slit almost all the way through, and I'm at the office alone. At least, I think I'm alone. Oh, my God. What if someone's here? I didn't look in any of the other offices. Whoever did this could still be here. Wait. You need an address. We're at…"

Laurel rattled off the address, finally managing to get to the corner of Brad's office so she could lean against the window. She went from wanting to cry to fighting the need to laugh hysterically at the ludicrous situation she'd found herself in all because she'd wanted to take home some files.

"Laurel, I'm sending units to your location now. Stay on the phone with me until…"

The 911 operator didn't have to worry about Laurel hanging up, because she needed someone to keep her somewhat sane. Her grip on the phone would probably leave an indentation. She was here in the same room with a dead body. And it was someone she knew well, and almost too well at that.

One would think she would be crying, but then again, she was still in shock. She kept waiting for someone to jump out from one of the offices down the long corridor and tell her that this was nothing more than some sick joke.

Brad Manon.

He was the man responsible for the entire trajectory of her career. He'd taken her on right out of college as a retail analyst, and she'd been working for Manon Investments for the last six years. She was making low six figures, with an opportunity to make more based on an offering of the upcoming partnership offer.

Oh, my God. I'm going to hell.

Laurel put a trembling hand over her mouth, wondering where her sense of compassion had gone in these last few minutes. Her boss, her mentor, had been killed in a horrible manner that she wouldn't wish on her worst enemy. Yet her thoughts had somehow drifted toward how this situation would impact her employment.

Yes, I'm going straight to hell.

"Laurel, are you still there?"

"Yes." She had to clear her throat a couple of times before she could get the word out, but it was as if she'd opened a dam. "I-I need to contact Paul. He's going to need to know what happened. So are the others. How am I going to explain any of this? How do I say Brad has been murdered? No one is going to believe me."

"Laurel, you can do all of that after the police arrive," the operator reassured her in a confident manner. It did nothing to alleviate the nausea that had taken up residence in her stomach. "Are you still in a position where you can see down the hallway? Is the door unlocked?"

"Yes," Laurel replied, furtively glancing down the dimly lit corridor. Her office provided most of the illumination, but there was track lighting that was left on during the evening hours. "I still don't see anyone, but I don't know how much longer I can stay—"

The echo of the glass door opening, followed by rapid footsteps, traveled down the still empty hallway. She gripped her cell phone harder to quell the fear bubbling up inside of her, only to sigh audibly with relief when she saw two men in uniform round the corner.

"The police are here," Laurel told the 911 operator in a rush, grateful that someone was here to take care of...Brad. She'd been trying her best not to look his way, but she was on the losing end of what she hoped was human nature. She would never get that sight out of her mind. "Thank you so much for staying on the line with me."

Laurel wasn't sure what the operator said in return, for she was focused on the two police officers coming through the door. One of them ushered her out of the office and escorted her to the reception area. She didn't challenge the direction, but the questions he began asking were somewhat overwhelming.

"Ma'am, are you Laurel Calanthe?" the officer asked, pulling out a small notebook. There was also a one-sided conversation being carried out in Brad's office, presumably the other officer reporting in to his station. "Are you the one who reported the body?"

The body.

The police officer meant Brad.

Laurel closed her eyes and breathed in deeply, trying to cull her erratic emotions. She was a career woman and could handle anything thrown her way. She repeated that several times in her mind, though she was pretty sure her daily mantra didn't extend to finding dead people.

"Okay," Laurel stated mostly to herself, somewhat better now that she was away from all the blood. She still couldn't prevent the shaking in her hands, but that was nothing a stiff shot of bourbon couldn't handle. Okay, a glass. Or two. "Yes, I'm Laurel Calanthe."

"Can you walk me through what happened?"

"I don't know what happened." Laurel was surprised to see

two paramedics walk through the glass door. Her line of sight followed them down the hallway. For a brief moment, she wondered if they thought Brad was alive. The vision of his throat slit came back in vivid colors, reminding her that wasn't the case. "Um, I came in to pick up some files and—"

"And what time was that?"

"Around one?" Laurel wasn't sure why she'd worded her statement as a question, considering she'd glanced at her watch in the elevator. She still had a death grip on her phone, so she pressed the home button. The display read one twenty-three. How had everything happened in the span on twenty-three minutes? "I saw Brad's light on in his office. I went to say hello and—"

"Was anyone with you?"

"No. I was on the phone with a colleague," Laurel replied, wishing he'd allow her to finish her sentences. She was feeling slightly better now that the copper smell wasn't so strong, and there was quite a lot she needed to do. Being busy would help her regain her equilibrium, as well. She glanced at his nametag. "Officer Dodds, I really need to contact Brad's partner. Paul needs to know what—"

"You said you were stopping by the office for some files." Officer Dodds nodded to another gentleman wearing an official-looking blazer who'd gotten off the elevator and was fixing the door so that it stayed open. A woman and another man followed closely behind, one with a black bag of some sort and another with a large camera. "Where were you this evening?"

The question had Laurel snapping her teeth together and closing her lips while she experienced a hot flash that was equal to being covered in lava.

This couldn't be happening.

First, Brad was brutally murdered. That in and of itself was going to send shockwaves through the company. At the foundation of every hedge fund was the portfolio manager. It was through his or her reputation that brought in the high net worth individuals. Brad's death could potentially mean the doors closing on Manon Investments.

But to throw in that she'd spent her evening in bed with the man who she was competing with for a partnership in said business would essentially be ending her career. She could have included Smith's career in that sentiment, but his family name and wealth would essentially wipe away any smear that could possibly stain his reputation.

Doubts began to swirl in the chaotic thoughts that had yet to settle down since she'd found Brad dead at his desk. What if Smith denied being with her this evening? What if he refused to give her an alibi? Should the company somehow survive if Paul took over as portfolio manager, or they brought someone new on board who had numbers to back up his or her performance, Smith would be a shoo-in for partnership while she'd be sitting behind bars wearing an orange jumpsuit.

"Ma'am?" Officer Dodds lifted the pen off the small pad of paper as he peered at her questioningly. "Are you okay? Do you need to sit down?"

"No," Laurel whispered, shaking her head to emphasize her answer. "No, I'm not okay."

CHAPTER TWO

S MITH GALLO WALKED past the crowd of people gathered in the foyer of the building. News reporters, police officers, various law enforcement support staff, and a couple of the building's own security guards were all broken off into groups and talking about what was about to hit the financial news first thing this morning. The industry would be reeling for weeks to come. The coverage of Brad Manon's death would dominate every outlet's talking head for less than half that time.

Brad hadn't been the easiest man to work with, though some would disagree with Smith's assessment on that front. The men had their differences. He'd only been working at Manon Investments for the last three years, unlike the majority of Brad's other employees. His run-ins with Brad had been like two bulls in a china shop sparring over which cup to break next. The business choices he'd been making lately had been beyond risky, even for a hedge fund.

"Excuse me," Smith said, brushing past a group of people gathered near the elevator bank.

"I'm sorry, sir." The officer who had been stationed to prevent people from accessing the elevators or stairwell held up a hand to prevent Smith from advancing. "Only authorized personnel past this point."

Smith clenched his jaw at the denial of entry, having learned long ago that all he had to do was toss his surname out into the wind to obtain anything he wanted. He also understood the value of hard work. He played by the rules for the most part, unlike the majority of his siblings.

In this case?

The rules would have to be broken.

"Detective Nielsen asked me to come down here to clear up some discrepancies." Smith smiled in confidence that this momentary delay would end quite soon. "I'm Smith Gallo, Judge Nathanial Gallo's son."

The officer hesitated briefly before stepping to the side. Smith used two fingers to press the correct floor number, doing his best not to show his impatience. It would serve him nothing but the attention of those leeches waiting to snap a picture of him. Those photographs would make it appear that he was tied to a particularly brutal murder, thereby smearing the family's name. It was only a matter of time before he received a call from his parents asking how he'd gotten tied up in all this rubbish.

Smith didn't react when he heard the officer radio to someone upstairs that they were about to have a guest. *Good.* Detective Nielsen was an upstanding officer, but the fact that a Gallo was in any way involved with a murder investigation would have him dotting every I and crossing every T in hopes of saving his own career.

Why had Laurel left his bed after midnight to return to the office? It would be the first truth Smith offered in hopes that he could clear up the mess she'd gotten herself into.

The elevator doors slid open and allowed him to disappear from the view of the media who'd now caught on to his presence thanks to the radio traffic. One reporter even called out his name, but he refused to look their way and give up the golden ticket for this morning's news. Within twenty seconds, he was granted access through the glass doors of Manon Investments.

"Mr. Gallo?"

Smith fleetingly spared a glance at the officer's nametag.

"Officer Dodds, please let Detective Nielsen know that I'm here per his request."

Smith stepped forward, his sole focus now on Laurel. She was sitting on the edge of a chair in the waiting area for clients, gripping her phone so tightly between her fingers that her knuckles were white. Her long chestnut waves hung over one shoulder, her second tell that let him know she was rattled. She tended to clear the soft strands off the back of her neck when she needed to think more clearly.

He didn't even need to speak her name for her to know that he'd arrived, because her green eyes made contact with him immediately…only to then have her gaze drift over his shoulder. He was confused as to why she looked so hesitant.

"Smith Gallo." Detective Nielsen's deep voice echoed through the corridor. "It's been a while since I last saw you. I'm sorry it had to be under these circumstances."

Smith shifted only slightly to ensure he could shake hands with the detective while allowing him to observe Laurel throughout the exchange. She'd definitely driven straight to the office from his bed, because she was still wearing the same slate grey business suit he'd removed himself earlier that night, stitch by stich. Her lips were void of the lipstick he'd kissed off with his own, and she didn't seem to notice that she was only sporting one earring. The other he'd inadvertently found on his bedroom floor when he'd gotten out of bed to go search for her.

"Detective," Smith greeted, having met the officer a couple of times over the years at various functions and charity balls thrown on behalf of the city's police department. "You have quite a crowd downstairs listening to your patrol officer's radio."

"Did those ears, by chance, perk up after they saw you walk through the front doors of the building?" Fred Nielsen frowned in displeasure at both assessments. It was obvious he didn't appreciate the rookie downstairs sharing any information through carelessness, but Fred also understood what would happens should the Gallo name be dragged into this murder investigation. "I explained on the phone that it would be in your best interest to stay away from this place for a few days. We could have had this discussion at your place, or better yet, at the station with your lawyer present. I'm well aware of how your father is going to want this handled."

"Nathaniel Gallo has nothing to do with this firm," Smith stressed, having fought this battle many times in the past. "I'm here to provide Laurel Calanthe an alibi. She was with me all evening, until around twelve-forty this morning when she left to come back here."

Smith didn't miss the way Laurel momentarily closed her eyes in what appeared to be relief. It was then he realized that she wasn't quite sure he'd tell the police the truth of her whereabouts. Red hot anger sliced through his pride. She had the temerity to question his integrity after occupying his bed for the last three months.

He wished like hell he could understand why he was drawn to her, of all people. She was unlike any other woman he'd ever come across in his thirty-one years. Hell, she'd even turned him down flat when he'd extended a dinner offer his first week at Manon Investments. And maybe that was the reason he couldn't get her out of his system.

He was addicted to her.

Laurel Calanthe was intelligent, driven, proud, and stunning-ly beautiful. She had an elegance that far surpassed the women who normally ran in his family's circle, yet she had an untapped wild side just waiting to be fed the right encouragement. Having her underneath him, on top of him, or basically anywhere he could manage to fuck her was a high he wasn't sure he could do without. And yet she didn't give a flying fuck who he was or what his surname could provide her in the long run. As a matter of fact, she treated his identity as almost a hindrance to their involvement.

"And your relationship with Ms. Calanthe?"

Smith experienced a shot of satisfaction when Laurel's lashes lifted in surprise at the question. Her natural lips parted as if she were going to deny that they had any type of relationship, but she was saved from making that mistake when her friend stopped her from speaking. It was a good thing that Grace Dorrance was seated in the chair next to Laurel in order to instill some form of reason.

"We're intimately involved, if that is in any way pertinent," Smith shared willingly with the detective, not concerned in the least that the truth was finally out in the open. It was abundantly apparent that he and Laurel weren't on the same page, but he was about to rectify that small problem. First, he needed to ensure that Laurel was no longer considered a prime suspect in the murder of their mutual boss. "It's my understanding that Brad Manon was murdered, but do you have any leads? I'm assuming you looked at all the surveillance feeds? I don't believe there is a square inch of this place that isn't monitored by some sort of a security camera."

"Thank you for your time, Mr. Gallo." The good detective obviously wasn't willing to share any details on the case. It wouldn't matter in the end, considering Smith's father would have complete access to all of the investigation's preliminary reports come sunrise. "You and Ms. Calanthe are free to go for now. I would like to question you both at some point tomorrow once we develop a timeline for the victim."

Laurel and Grace were in what appeared to be a heated yet whispered conversation, but they both became quiet as he walked away from the detective to stand before them.

"I appreciate you coming here to confirm my whereabouts." Laurel gave him a smile of gratitude, though she still maintained an aloofness that rubbed him the wrong way, considering the recent efforts on her part. She even squared her shoulders as she began listing things that had no bearing on what she'd gone through this evening. "Grace and I have spent the last thirty minutes calling Paul, Cynthia, Vern, and Steve. Cynthia will notify the rest of the employees. Obviously, Paul should be arriving here shortly. We can't shut down trading, especially with those option trades of yours about to expire. We can—"

"Grace, would you please excuse us?" Smith asked, not bothering to remove his suit jacket. He and Laurel wouldn't be here long enough to warrant taking it off, anyway. "I'd like to have a word with Laurel in private."

"Of course," Grace murmured, running her palms over the rough denim of her jeans. Smith had never seen the woman in anything other than a business suit or something equally as formal, so it had taken him a moment to realize that it was her who had been sitting next to Laurel. "I'm going to go make us some coffee. That is, if they let me in the kitchen area."

Smith waited for Grace to leave before kneeling in front of Laurel, who seemed quite taken aback by his casual intimacy. The simmering anger he'd experienced was still there, right at the level where he could still control the words coming out of his mouth. He'd deal with that later, but she'd experienced a trauma that one didn't just get over in the span of two hours.

"Are you okay?"

Laurel inhaled deeply, albeit her breathing was a bit erratic.

She glanced up at the ceiling in an attempt to maintain control over her emotions. Couldn't she see that he was there for her or that it was okay to let down her guard for just a moment?

"Honestly, I think I'm still in a bit of shock." Laurel cleared her throat before attempting to divert attention away from herself. "I left a voicemail for Meredith, but I didn't go into detail. I feel as if one of us should go over to her house, but the detective assured me that it was proper protocol for him to send an officer instead. Maybe that's why Paul isn't here yet. Maybe he went over to Meredith's residence to tell her what happened."

Meredith Manon was Brad's ex-wife, though the two had remained friends over the years. Of course, Detective Nielsen would want to speak with her, considering she was about to inherit a not-so-small fortune. The spouse, or ex-spouse in this case, was always the prime suspect in any homicide.

"I'm asking if *you* are okay, Laurel." Smith could only imagine what it was like for her to find Brad dead at his desk. "I know you were fond of Brad. I'm sorry you had to find him like you did."

Laurel finally gave him all her attention, and it was the first time he'd ever seen her truly vulnerable with her emotions racing. Even in the throes of passion, she kept some measure of reserve. Now, her eyes filled with tears, though they didn't spill over her lashes. She'd even let go of her phone and grabbed his hand instead, but in the next moment it was as if nothing had passed between them.

"Paul," Laurel exclaimed, abruptly standing and all but forcing Smith to do the same. She stepped away from him to put distance between them, letting him know exactly where he stood in the grand scheme of things. That talk he'd put off for her benefit was going to come sooner rather than later. "I'm so sorry. I know the last thing you want to deal with is the business, but Cynthia is already reaching out to the clients. If there's anything that I can do to help, please let me know."

"I just can't believe this is happening," Paul stated in somewhat shock, nodding toward Smith in an odd questioning manner. Apparently, his presence wasn't expected. "I would have been here sooner, but the officer downstairs wouldn't allow me to come up until he'd checked with the detective in charge. Grace told me you'd stopped into the office to grab some files and found Brad with his throat cut. I just can't—"

Paul's voice caught, and he shook his head in remorse. He took an unsteady breath.

"You've seen and done enough tonight." Paul rested a hand on Laurel's shoulder in appreciation and support. It was a familiar gesture that Smith wasn't altogether comfortable with. "Go home. Get some rest. The upcoming few days are going to be hell as we try to figure out what happens next."

"Mr. Slater?" Detective Nielsen interrupted, all business and looking as if he needed a cup of that coffee Grace had gone to make. "I'd like to make arrangements to question all of your employees. I understand it's a Saturday, but it would make it easier to use an office here rather than dragging them down to the station at different times."

"Paul," Laurel said softly, preventing the man from answering the detective. She didn't meet Smith's questioning gaze. "There's something I need to tell you."

"Can it wait?" Paul asked, a frown marring his weathered face. He'd just come back from a trip to the Caribbean, where the office's offshore accounts were set up with financial institutions for non-U.S. clients. He usually made the trip annually for compliance purposes. He'd gone more often in the past two years. "I have a lot to deal with right now, Laurel."

Smith finally understood the reason for Laurel's unease. She wanted Paul to hear from her where she'd been for most of last night before hearing about it from the police. He didn't take her as the shallow type, but it was evident that she was concerned with her position here at Manon Investments. She was equally troubled about their intimate relationship going public. It was time they discuss both.

"Detective, I can have Cynthia Ellsworth set up a rotation starting at seven o'clock this morning. Cynthia is our compliance officer, and she'll have…"

Paul's voice trailed off as Detective Nielsen guided him toward the other side of the large office space to where the trading area was located, overlooking part of the city. The reception area was the heart of the design, setting up several offices down another corridor to their right. Smith would have taken Laurel to his office to have their private conversation, but a forensics team was currently occupying his professional domain. He wasn't worried in the least and would deal with any outcome at a later date.

"You're pale and running on lack of sleep." Smith was done handling her with kid gloves. She wanted things between them to remain status quo, but the cat was out of the bag. There was no going back, but there were two paths ahead of them. "Let's get you back to my place where you can get some rest. I'm sure Cynthia will contact us in the morning with a time assigned for our talk with Detective Nielsen."

"Smith, this doesn't change—"

"If you're about to stand there and tell me that this situation doesn't alter the nature of our relationship, then you're sorely mistaken." Smith wrapped his hand around Laurel's upper arm, pulling her close so that no one else heard their private conversation. There was something else that needed to be addressed. "And don't think for a moment I didn't see the surprise written across those beautiful features of yours when I gave you an alibi. You actually thought I would hang you out to dry, didn't you, you little minx?"

CHAPTER THREE

LAUREL ALLOWED HERSELF to have a mini-breakdown, not that she did it in front of Smith. He'd finally taken her home to his apartment, neither one saying a word during the entire drive. There was nothing either of them needed to say.

Yes, they were competitors. Had she had a sliver of doubt that he would bend the truth in such a manner that it would benefit his career? Of course, she had her doubts. She'd been in the industry long enough to know that nearly anyone within arm's reach of a sturdy blade would stab another in the back to gain advantage. And that self-same analogy was what had her on the brink of tears before they'd even pulled into the underground garage.

She half-jokingly told Grace that she was going to hell. Like a true friend, Grace had told her that she would be waiting for her with a piping hot cup of coffee. Unfortunately, that short-lived moment of humor didn't take away from the grim reality that someone they'd come to respect had died in the most brutal fashion imaginable.

"Are you feeling any better?"

Laurel startled when Smith's voice came from somewhere across the bedroom. It was still dark outside, and he hadn't turned on his bedside lamp. Her eyes slowly adjusted from the well-lit bathroom to the darkness to find that he was leaning against the window frame with a half-full rocks glass in his hand, minus the rocks, of course. From the darker shadow cast by the liquid glimmering in the moonlight, it had to be his favorite brand of single malt whiskey—Glenglassaugh thirty-year-old scotch direct from the Highlands.

How was it that this man could be so close to perfection? His chiseled features were sharp, yet commanding. The muscles running alongside his jaw were usually taut and made a woman want to press her palm against his cheek to offer him some measure of relaxation. He radiated a self-assuredness through each measured motion, which was the attribute that landed her in his bedroom to begin with.

She'd closed all but one button on the white Egyptian cotton collar of his Joseph Abboud dress shirt, grateful that he'd put something out on the sink for her to wear. It was one that he'd worn, and it smelled of his Jaipur cologne. She always made sure never to leave anything of hers at his place for obvious reasons. No one was ever supposed to know they were involved, so she had no change of clothes nor did she have any of her makeup, other than the few touchup items that were in her purse. That hadn't stopped her from taking a hot shower the moment they'd walked through his door. She needed to be clean.

"No, not really," Laurel replied honestly, shutting off the bathroom light before stepping farther into the bedroom. She wasn't sure why she'd allowed him to talk her into coming to his place instead of grabbing her own keys and driving herself to her apartment. She chalked it up to weakness, allocating herself just a bit in a crisis like this. "I'm not okay. He—"

The initial shock value of what she'd found at the office was wearing off, leaving her in the midst of an emotional turmoil. Brad was dead. He'd been killed in the most horrific manner possible, and she couldn't stop her mind from processing the fear he must have felt during those precious few seconds knowing that his mortality was slipping away with each spurt of his life's blood.

Laurel had cried for the man who'd given her a chance at succeeding in the financial industry, she wept for a friendship that had grown distant over the years, and she continued to shed tears for what the public would do to his legacy after word got out about his murder. It wasn't until the water began to cool in the shower that she'd been able to collect her wits.

"I honestly don't know what to feel right now. I still can't believe I found him like that." Laurel walked to the bed she'd spent countless hours in, especially as of late. She curled her left leg under her as she sank into the most comfortable mattress she'd ever laid on, whether sleeping or not. It reminded her that the situation she currently found herself in wasn't the norm. They had sex. Hot sex. But they were always careful to never let it turn or allow it to cross over into their personal lives, and she didn't want him to feel like he was responsible for her. "Smith, I can call a cab. There's no reason for me to stay here."

Laurel had spent her childhood watching her mother work two jobs and raise a child by herself, all the while taking night classes to get her bachelor's degree in business almost too late to use it. Brenda Calanthe finally managed to climb that mountain of success, having done so all by herself with very little help from anyone. Never once had she permitted anyone to show her pity in regard to her situation. If anything, that kind of patronizing sentiment gave her the will to push herself to the finish line.

Had Smith brought her here because he felt sorry for her that she'd been the one to find Brad with his throat slit? She didn't need him to serve her a dose of sympathy. Their relationship didn't extend to mollycoddling the distressed maiden, and she certainly didn't want him to do so out of some wrong sense of obligation.

"You truly believe that, don't you?" Smith asked in that aloof manner of his when something angered him. She'd seen this dismissive demeanor time and again when someone in the office did something to piss him off, though he'd never before been this way with her. The thud of his now empty crystal glass on the granite window ledge echoed throughout his bedroom, the sudden noise causing her heartbeat to accelerate. "You've willingly spent the last three months in my bed. You requested to keep our relationship private for your own reasons. We only ever come to my place, never yours, and you never stay the full night. You never go into detail about your childhood, and you always manage to divert the conversation to business if it touches on anything remotely personal. So, what happens? I ask how you're doing, and you want to call a fucking cab? This is beyond unbelievable."

Laurel wasn't sure how this conversation went from her mental health to the confidential affair they'd *both* agreed to keep quiet. Okay, so she told Grace due to the context. And Cynthia, who as their compliance officer about had a coronary. But none of that mattered, because this…*thing*…between her and Smith wasn't going anywhere in reality. It couldn't, because she wouldn't let it.

She slowly rose from the bed, allowing her anger to do the same. She'd been through hell tonight, and he was upset because she wanted to call a cab so that she could manage a few hours of sleep in her own bed. Another stab of guilt that she was thinking of herself when Brad was dead only fueled the rage building up inside of her.

"Is this some sort of retort due to the fact that you had to give me an alibi?" Laurel fully understood the ramifications of his statement, but she wasn't taking the blame for circumstances beyond her control. "Smith, I had no choice but to honestly inform the police where I was last night. It was easy to determine where the police were leading me with their line of questioning, especially given the fact that I was the one who'd found Brad dead in his office at one o'clock in the morning."

"You mean the alibi that you had doubts I would back up?" There was a warning somewhere in the tone of Smith's voice, but Laurel chose to ignore the blaring sirens. He'd have to explain himself a bit better if he wanted her to understand why he was angry with her. "Do you really think so little of me? Am I completely devoid of character in your eyes?"

"Is that what this whole tantrum is all about?" Laurel asked with disbelief, reaching for the bedside lamp. Smith had stepped away from the window with a sudden quickness. She'd always known he had a dangerous side to him, but he'd never turned it on her. Now? She could all but feel the underlying anger radiating off his body. "Why would I think anything else, Smith? You could have easily said we weren't together at all, casting suspicion on me while gaining favor with the board. That partnership would have been yours, and you knew that going in."

"Are you suggesting that you wouldn't have had my back if the roles were reversed?"

"Of course, I would have given you an alibi," Laurel exclaimed, wishing he'd stop advancing to her side of the room in a series of exaggerated small rushes. She didn't care for his aggressive manner. His dress shirt was undone, revealing a contoured abdomen that didn't get that way by merely going to the gym. She had no idea what he did in his spare time, and she'd always been careful not to ask too many personal questions. But she wasn't about to be distracted by sex after the night she'd had or the day that remained ahead of her. "It's not the same thing, though."

Laurel was finally realizing that she'd missed something major between leaving his bed last night and him all but being forced to admit that they were having an affair. Smith's brown eyes darkened to almost black as he curled the fingers of his right hand into a fist and raised it in the air. He shook his head in frustration and then began to emphasize a couple of points that she'd purposefully ignored over the last three months.

"It's not the same because of who you think I am? Because I'm a Gallo?" Smith took another step forward and pointed an accusing finger her way. "You have absolutely no idea who I really am, do you? I've shown you, night after night, in *that* fucking bed. And yet you never looked beyond the fact that the sex met your requirements. You never once *wanted* to see who I was, because then that would mean letting me see *you* for who you truly are."

"Stop emphasizing your words that way," Laurel practically cried out, wishing more than anything she could go back to last night when she was driving away from his place. She never would have stopped at the office, she never would have needed an alibi, and this conversation would never have taken place. "We both agreed to keep things uncomplicated…casual. Don't you dare go and turn this around on me like I'm some heartless witch."

Laurel held up a hand when Smith took another step, bringing him even closer than he was before. The trembling she'd experienced earlier at the office had returned, but this time it wasn't in fear. It was spurred by anger. Well, it was and it wasn't. He was getting the reaction he obviously wanted, but that was the problem. What did he want from her?

"Oh, no, sweetheart." Smith seemed to have himself back under control, but that's what scared her the most. He was always full of confidence, but he now had it in spades. It was as if he'd just conquered the prey he'd been after for a very long time. "I followed your lead on this one, because it was the only way to get you into my bed. And this? The fire I see in your eyes right now? She was well worth the wait."

Laurel had always prided herself on maintaining her composure through thick and thin. She never allowed her emotions to conquer her will, yet here she was raising her voice and reacting recklessly to his barbed accusations. And it was all because she'd found the dead body of her boss.

"You know what?"

Laurel unbuttoned his shirt she was wearing, albeit jerkily because of all the adrenaline coursing through her veins. She refused to stay here another minute. It was more than obvious they needed some time apart, so she'd be the smart one and simply walk away. How she managed to botch her planned exit was beyond her, but it all started when she began to verbalize her thoughts. Later, she'd realize that's why spinsters had cats.

"I don't need this crap." Laurel could see she'd surprised Smith with her declaration. Well, he could join the club. She'd even managed to get stuck on the last button, causing her to take it off over her head before shoving the shirt into his chest. "I'm already going to hell. Do you know what thought first crossed my mind when I realized Brad was dead? That I wouldn't get the partnership I'd worked my ass off for the last six years. Who does that? Someone going straight to hell, that's who."

"Laurel, you—"

"On top of that?" Laurel began walking toward the bathroom where she'd left her clothes, but she spun back around to finish the speech she should have never given breath to in the first place. "I'm sleeping with *you*! A man who is definitely way out of my league and a colleague with whom I should have stuck to my original answer that I gave regarding your first invitation.

But I didn't do that, did I? No, I had to have sex with you, didn't I? Oh, and it had to be good sex. Great sex, as a matter of fact! Probably the best sex I've ever had, and look at me now. I'm all fucked up."

Laurel began counting off the negatives by raising a finger for each one.

"No partnership. Our boss is dead. You had to give me an alibi for the murder that everyone is going to hear about. In fact, everyone is going to know we're having sex by six o'clock this morning because of said alibi. We're probably both out of a job, give or take a year or however long it's going to take to close the funds. And…oh, yeah. I'm going to hell!"

Laurel held up a hand with all five fingers displayed, not expecting him to latch on to her wrist and yank her up against him. What air she did have left in her lungs after allowing the verbal dam to break came out in a whoosh, taking all her anger with it.

He was touching her face, making this personal. She'd always maintained her composure around him, but his easy acceptance of their affair being made public had crumbled the barriers she always had in place.

"You're changing our rules," Laurel whispered, tears burning the back of her eyes. She blinked furiously to get them to go away, but the gentle touch of his palm against her cheek made that impossible. "You don't get to change the rules like that."

"Sweetheart, I hate to break this to you," Smith murmured, his lips barely an inch from hers. The heat coming from his body had hers responding in kind. "But I *made* the rules, so I can break them."

CHAPTER FOUR

L AUREL WAS GOING to combust from a single kiss.

It was wrong on so many levels.

They shouldn't be having sex the morning after their boss was murdered. It wasn't right, respectful, or even remotely acceptable. Why, then, did she part her lips wanting more?

He tasted of whiskey. She could always blame the alcohol, but she didn't think that would fly in the grand scheme of things. He ran his tongue across her lower lip after stating he'd made the rules of this game they were in, almost as if he were hypnotizing her with his flavor. Maybe he was.

"We shouldn't…"

Laurel gasped in response when Smith took her arm and pinned it against her lower half. He was usually a gentle lover, thoroughly loving every inch of her body before taking his own pleasure. Yes, there were times when the sex needed to be fast and hot, but she'd always been equally rushed on those occasions.

"My rules." Smith lightly bit her lower lip, but yet hard enough to leave a stinging sensation that blossomed into a burning arousal. He raised his head and met her gaze, momentarily paralyzing her with his simmering intensity. Her nipples hardened against his chest. "But we'll have to go over those changes later. Right now, I want you."

Smith continued to walk them toward the bed, not stopping

until she was laying on the comforter with him standing over her. His dark gaze traveled the length of her body as he shrugged out of his dress shirt, letting it drop to the floor. She was used to the rising heat in this bedroom, but something was different this time…the rules. And she wasn't sure how to change them back.

"Put both your hands above your head." Laurel would have laughed had she not sensed his authority surrounding her. The nerves in her body began to awaken at his introduction, all but telling her that this was what she wanted from him. She didn't try to fight her own needs. "Leave them there."

Laurel wanted to ask what he would do should she go against that directive, but his knee sinking into the mattress beside her stole her breath. His was imposing dressed, but he was all man in the nude. The faint hint of his cologne surrounded her as he leaned down and pressed his warm lips against the side of her neck. She let her head fall to the side in acceptance.

She would allow this momentary lapse of control because she needed the intimacy his touch could provide. She needed to feel something other than the consuming fear and horror she'd experienced earlier that morning. The brush of his fingers against the side of her breast had her arching for more than a mere caress.

Smith answered her unspoken plea by trailing his lips down the curve of her shoulder, over the swell of her flesh, and closing them over her highly sensitive nipple. She cried out when his tongue stroked over the stiff tip. The overwhelming sensation had her capturing his dark hair in between her fingers.

Immediately, a rush of cool air hit her nipple when he raised his head. The heat within his gaze was likely to catch her body on fire and burn them both down.

"Put your hands back where they were, sweetheart." Smith shifted both of them so that her head was on the pillow. He then whispered into her ear. "I'm not going to tell you again."

Laurel sunk her fingers deep into the goose down pillow as Smith began to have his way with her. There were no other words to describe the way his lips, tongue, and teeth pleasured her with no opposition in his way. By the time he made it back to her nipples, she was on the verge of an orgasm of epic proportions.

"You hold back." At first, Laurel thought she'd only imagined hearing those words. She was so caught up in what his fingers were doing to her nipples that all she could hear was her own labored breathing. "Every time you come for me, you hold a piece of yourself back. Not tonight."

Smith pinched both of her nipples hard enough to chase away the panic that threatened to consume her with his intense observation. Sharp arousal spread from her breasts to her clitoris, where her pussy was now throbbing in aching need. She didn't hesitate to part her thighs when his right hand began to travel lower. She wanted more. She needed more.

"I want you to feel every stroke of my fingers and every lick of my tongue."

Laurel wasn't so sure he hadn't lit a match to her fuse. His fingertips barely brushed over her clit, but the feather light touch sent tingling heat straight to her core. She bit her lip to keep from crying out. It was obvious that she was wet from the way his finger slid so easily inside her folds. Unfortunately, he didn't quite give her body what it needed.

"You're still holding back, Laurel." Smith nipped the sensitive skin on her inner thigh, having moved farther down to settle himself between her legs. "I want to hear you scream my name. I want my neighbors to know who's giving you all this pleasure."

Smith spread her folds until she was open to him, the swipe of his tongue almost painful against the sensitive ball of tissue.

She moaned her pleasure, not sure why that wasn't enough for him. She barely had any sensation left in her hands from how tightly they dug into the pillow for support. When he suckled her engorged clit into his mouth, she squeezed her elbows around her ears to try and lessen the ringing that had set up permanent residence inside her head.

Her orgasm was seconds away.

"Don't you come for me just yet, sweetheart." Smith pulled away from her, causing her to release a groan of frustration. "I'm nowhere near done with you, so you settle back and enjoy the journey."

"Smith, just get on with it," Laurel pleaded, done with whatever point he was trying to make. Her body couldn't take much more of this foreplay.

"This," Smith said, surprising her when he was suddenly on top of her. The palm of his hand cupped her pussy, capturing her warmth. "Will never. Be. Over."

Laurel parted her lips in surprise when his middle finger slid through her folds and entered her wet sheath until his fingertip rested on her sweet spot. He didn't move it, but instead, waited until she met his heated gaze. There was an underlying excitement in his dark eyes, almost as if he was daring her to release the pillow behind her head.

The need to come overshadowed her need to rebel against his declaration.

Smith stayed where he was, watching her closely as he began to thrust his finger in and out of her pussy. He somehow managed to graze that same small sensitive area over and over again in a steady rhythm that had her mind being carried away in a steady current of escalating stimulation.

"More?" Smith leaned down to capture her lips before he used her cream to aid another finger in joining the first. It was more pressure. Intense pleasure. "Widen your legs for me, Laurel. Take what I'm giving you."

Laurel found that her body was automatically responding to his commands before she could even think about what he said. She dug her heels into the soft comforter, using the mattress underneath as leverage. She opened herself for him, a short cry escaping before she could stop it. He'd added a third finger and pressed firmly on her clit with his thumb.

The first contraction of her sheath closed around his fingers. His knee over hers prevented her from closing her legs. She was going to explode into a million pieces.

"Look at me."

Laurel wasn't sure why this moment was different from all the others.

"Come."

Against her own will, her body followed his resolute command. It was almost painful the way he drew out her orgasm, the pads of his three fingers continually stroking her sweet spot. She stared up into his dark eyes filled with burning desire. She wanted…needed…him to bring her down from his masterpiece of foreplay.

"Smith!" Laurel broke their connection when she arched in response to his thumb pressing harder on her clit. He wasn't stopping the combined, talented manipulations. If anything, he was drawing out her release. "Please, please…"

Something extraordinary happened.

Smith withdrew his fingers, but he began to softly rub her moisture over her clit in circles over and over again until another stronger orgasm took hold of her body with massive contractions. This time there was no holding back. She screamed his name and succumbed to the overpowering eruption.

CHAPTER FIVE

" I DIDN'T CALL for a lecture."

Smith had no choice but to set boundaries for this phone call. He understood his father all too well, and they'd gone head to head many times in the past. The first real showdown had been regarding his switch from law to business when he'd attended Harvard University. The threats of being cut off from the family trust fund had made him realize just how shallow and materialistic the Gallos family had become over the years.

Well, that crap ended with him.

"I'm sure you saw the news this morning regarding Brad Manon's murder." Smith didn't doubt for a moment that Nathanial Gallo had been given every detail before then calling his contacts at the police station to obtain the rest of the story. "Manon Investments will no doubt be closing their doors within the next year. Who would benefit from that?"

Smith poured coffee into the two cups that were positioned on either side of the plate he'd filled with fresh fruit and toast. He and Laurel were due at the office to speak with Detective Nielsen at ten o'clock. It was only now going on eight. That left them enough time to clear any misconceptions she had about last night and what had, in fact, changed.

"It's my understanding that no one would benefit from Manon Investments going under—not even Paul Slater, his partner." Nathaniel Gallo wasn't one to mince words. "I've already spoken with the police chief. Apparently, Brad Manon had some gambling debt. Quite a lot of money, from what I understand. It wouldn't surprise me if he got involved with the wrong sort of people."

That was Nathaniel's way of saying that Smith had gotten involved with the wrong kind of people himself. Well, he wasn't going to take the bait. His parents were in for quite a shock as it was when he brought Laurel to the charity dinner they were hosting soon. In his best estimate, it would be the perfect time to go public with their relationship, especially given that the now defunct partnership slot no longer required them to be discreet. He'd kept this quiet based on her wishes, but that had changed after last night's usual tryst and their subsequent encounters with the police.

"Is that what the intrepid Detective Nielsen believes?" Smith asked, reaching into the refrigerator for the half and half he kept on hand for Laurel's visits. She was never around in the mornings to drink coffee, but once in a while they enjoyed a cup after a private dinner or between rendezvouses. "What about Manon's ex-wife? Did she have some type of outstanding life insurance policy out on him?"

"Manon did have a life insurance policy, but it was barely enough to cover the mortgage on the house she was encumbered with after the divorce." Nathanial didn't waste time getting to the root of his call. There were only two reasons Smith had answered his cell phone in the first place. One had been he didn't want the noise to wake up Laurel, and the second was that his father would have vital information on an investigation that would impact both Smith and Laurel. "Listen, now might be the time where you reevaluate your choices, son. You have—"

"You're right," Smith said, cutting off his father from taking the conversation into territory he believed would lead them both over a cliff. "It is time for me to reevaluate, which is why I'll be contacting each and every one of our investors to let them know they'll have a place to invest their money with my firm. I would never have extended such an offer, but in light of certain circumstances, that landscape has changed. I'm sure that puts me in the suspect pool, but my lawyer can handle that."

"Your *own* investment firm?" Smith's father seemed to mull over that idea, allowing the words to roll off his tongue. He had taken issue with the fact that Smith had wanted to work for someone else in the beginning, rather than take the reins and have his own surname on the door. It wasn't a surprise that he would now reassess the advantages and disadvantages of having his youngest son branch out on his own. "This might—"

"You were going to quit?" Laurel's voice was loud enough that his father stopped speaking on the other end of the line. She was standing in the doorway of the bedroom, looking like temptation incarnate wearing nothing but the white dress shirt he'd given her last night. From the daggers shooting from those marvelous green eyes of hers, he could easily distinguish that she was also mad as hell. The combination had him hardening, reminding him that he hadn't taken his pleasure before she'd all but fallen into a vegetative state after reaching hers. "When were you going to tell me this? After you won the partnership, leaving me high and dry with nothing?"

"Dad, I'll have to call you back." Smith disconnected the line before his father could get another word in edgewise. He gently set his phone on the counter by the breakfast tray he'd put together, accepting that his vision of gradually waking her by running a fresh-cut strawberry across her pink lips wasn't going to materialize. "Laurel, it was always my intention to gain enough experience before managing my own fund. The partnership meant nothing to me, and I would have refused had Brad or Paul offered it to me. It was yours all along to accept or reject."

Smith was only wearing trousers. He'd had every intention of climbing back into bed with her after speaking with his father, but that was looking more and more unlikely as the flush rose higher on her cheeks. He leaned back against the counter.

It was time they both laid their cards on the table.

"Mine?" Laurel took a step forward, pointing a French manicured fingernail his way. Her gorgeous tresses were tousled while her lips were still slightly swollen from their earlier tryst. "Do you realize that I put in more hours over the last three months than I have the last year? I've been running on four hours of sleep between analyzing companies, sitting in on various board meetings, and having sex with your traitorous ass."

"Great sex, might I reiterate," Smith reminded her with a small smile, throwing her own words back in her face. He held up a hand when she advanced another step. *Okay.* She wasn't ready to allow him to lighten the mood. He was fine with that, but he'd wait until she was closer before proving she was right. "I touched base with Cynthia. We're to be at the office this morning."

"We?" Laurel was already shaking her head to the contrary, pushing aside his attempt to change the subject. "I'll speak to Cynthia myself regarding my interview with Detective Nielsen. *We* won't be doing anything together. This…"

"Great sex?" Smith offered, filling in her words when she kept circling her finger to encompass what was between them. He was no longer smiling. She didn't get to end *this*. "Lovers? Relationship?"

"We both decided to keep things casual, so don't you dare

stand there and make this out to be more than it really is." Laurel took another step closer as she attempted to disengage from the bond that had grown between them. "We always understood where the line was drawn in the sand, and neither of us were allowed to cross it. This was always meant to be a temporary alliance. I was going to tell you yesterday after work, but…"

Laurel didn't have to finish her description of what had taken place the moment she'd walked through his door yesterday evening. Of course, that was before she decided to sneak out after midnight while he was asleep to avoid his usual request that she spend the night.

He'd taken a shower before her arrival and had answered the door with nothing but a towel around his waist. The large cotton cloth had still been left by the front door when he'd walked out after receiving the call informing him that Brad Manon was dead and the police needed to corroborate Laurel's whereabouts—which she'd actually had the balls to question him on whether or not he would lie about such a thing.

"You were going to tell me that we were over?" Smith kept his tone even, wondering how he would have played that scenario out had she actually attempted to end their relationship. He could still hear his name falling from her lips after pleasuring her. No. Things between them were far from over. She was in denial. One important detail needed to be addressed before moving on to another. "Laurel, what misconception makes you believe that I'm out of your league?"

Smith truly wanted to hear how she could arrive at that conclusion, when he'd done everything in his power to even the playing field from the very beginning.

"Why? Because I went to an Ivy League school? I graduated with a business degree, worked at two investment companies over the span of ten years, and managed to pay my father back for every penny he put into my highly overpriced education. Is it anything you see in this apartment?" It was Smith's turn to wave his hand at their surroundings, but he was very measured in how he spoke. This was not the time to lose the upper hand. "I bought every item with the money I earned from the long hours I've spent learning the way the gears grind in the financial industry—the mechanisms of making money. Being a Gallo has been nothing but a hindrance ever since I've tried to break out on my own, but you wouldn't understand that, would you? Because you never bothered to look beyond the *great sex*. So let me ask you now that you're beginning to understand where I'm coming from. What could possibly make you imagine that I'm out of your league?"

"Since when did you want anything more than a quick fuck?" Laurel had purposely devalued what was between them, but Smith let it go with an annoyed grimace. He could see the panic written across her features that they were once again entering territory she usually shied away from. "You can't rewrite our history, Smith."

"I might not be able to rewrite your understanding of history, but I can damn well set the course for our future together on a different path."

"Our future?" Laurel gave a disbelieving laugh and must have decided the distance between them was causing a problem with their communication. She finally took those last few steps to get her point across. "We don't have a future, Smith. Brad's murder put that azimuth one hundred and eighty degrees out…that changed everyone's future. Regardless of the fact that you were going to resign from the company, Manon Investments will close their doors. I'll probably end up going to New York, while you stay here and pretend you're not a Gallo. Speaking of which, that is exactly why you're out of my league, so don't pretend to be dense, Harvard boy. I don't run in your family's circles. I will never run in those mythical social microcosms, just as you would never set foot in my old working-class neighborhood. I worked through my high school years, Smith, just so I could buy clothes that weren't from a secondhand shop. I worked through college so that I could have a car and lived off of ramen noodles instead of spending my last few dollars on nights out. I didn't accomplish all of that just to throw it all away on…"

"Great sex?" Smith experienced a bit of déjà vu when he reached out to wrap his fingers around her wrist, but they no longer had time for what usually transpired afterward. That didn't stop him from pulling her forward, using her momentum to spin them around so that she was pinned against the granite countertop. He leaned down so that they were eye to eye and she couldn't misinterpret anything he said or take it out of context. "You've told me more about yourself in the last minute than you have in the past three months that you've occupied my bed, so let me share a bit about myself. I gave you those three months to get used to the idea of us, Laurel, because I realized from the first time you said no that you weren't like the other women who only wanted what my name could provide. With each day that passed, I noticed you called the mail boy by his name, treated every employee as if they were as important as the CEO, and never stabbed anyone in the back…even when the SOBs deserved it."

"So you think you want something more than sex because I'm nice to the mail boy?"

Laurel stressed her question as if it were inconceivable, causing another rush of anger to course through his veins. She was either purposefully being obtuse to what he was saying or he hadn't chipped away nearly enough cement from those walls she'd put up around her heart. From the defensive way she had her arms crossed in front of her waist, he guessed the former. After all, she'd all but surrendered in his arms last night. Which meant he needed to spell it out for her so that there were no more misunderstandings.

"You were never a *quick fuck* to me, sweetheart." Smith leaned in a bit closer to drive his point home. "You were always meant to be mine."

CHAPTER SIX

"I DON'T REALLY have to ask where you went, but it would have been nice to have a heads up before you disappeared on the same night our boss was murdered," Grace muttered, walking up to Laurel with a hot cup of coffee. Grace handed off the black porcelain mug before giving Phil Colbert a deadly stare. The technology analyst continued walking toward the office set up for interviews, while Laurel and Grace remained in the foyer. "On the bright side, Smith Gallo certainly saved your ass, in spite of who and what he is. It might be in your best interest to stay with him for another week or two. That way, he won't retract his alibi."

"That's not even remotely close to being funny." Laurel eyed her friend over the rim of her cup, downing a good bit of the contents before realizing it was black. No sugar, no half and half. The coffee hadn't been meant for her. She spit half of it back into the mug. "What's been going on here with the investigation?"

Did it make her a bad person to want to talk about the death of her boss over her personal life? She'd already accepted her fate, so she might as well stay the course.

"Have they removed his body? Have the police figured out who killed him?"

Laurel couldn't believe an arrest hadn't been made yet. There were video cameras everywhere in this place. The killer had to have been recorded on one of the backup discs.

Her chest tightened at the memory of what Brad looked like sitting in his chair with his throat slit—the way his eyes were glazed over looking so dull and the general expression of horror written across his still features. It would haunt her for the rest of her life.

"The coroner took his body out of the office around six o'clock this morning. Forensics left about an hour ago." Grace spared a glance toward Marilyn, their receptionist who was in her mid-sixties and had ears sharper than a jackrabbit. "I don't think the police know exactly who did it, which is why we're being paraded into that office as if we're nothing more than a herd of cattle being led to the slaughter."

"It's more like roulette. That detective has been spinning the wheel, seeing who lands in the guilty slot." Cynthia appeared out of nowhere before wrapping an arm around Laurel's shoulders. The silver bracelets lightly chimed with the woman's graceful movements. "You doing okay, doll? Grace said you'd gone home with a man who I shall not name. I figured he'd put you to bed. A first for everything, but this does call for extenuating circumstances."

"Would you two just stop?" Laurel whispered harshly, chastising both of them for making assumptions. It didn't matter that she'd done the same, though Smith's affirmation that she was his to keep had been a bit presumptuous. Nothing he said or did last night changed anything about who they were, regardless of how her body responded to his. She shook her head, realizing that she was getting off track herself. "Nothing showed up on the security cameras? How is that possible?"

"They were wiped clean. No recording on any of the DVDs. They were all unformatted blanks. Whoever had access to the building after hours was somehow able to disable the surveillance system since five o'clock yesterday afternoon and replace the system's recording with blanks from our own supply." Grace shrugged when both Laurel and Cynthia looked at her in surprise. "What? Marilyn's not the only one who pays attention. Besides, I was first up to be interviewed. Who knew the office walls were so thin?"

"Did Grace tell you that I'm going to hell?" Laurel lifted the coffee to her lips despite the fact that Grace had given her acid in a cup. She managed another sip without a grimace or spitting it back out. "Brad's dead, and all I could think about was *bye-bye* partnership."

"That's human nature," Cynthia said in understanding, brushing aside her concern for the fact that her friend would burn in hell for all eternity. "And it would be totally different had Brad been the same man he was when Manon Investments started out how many years ago? Let's face it. He'd let greed change him, and not for the better. Honestly, he had turned into a dick. Death doesn't change the facts of who he was."

"Cynthia's right," Grace acknowledged, leaning back a bit so she could see down the long hallway. Laurel flicked her gaze in that direction, having already noted the yellow crime scene tape. Her stomach rolled and threatened to empty its contents at the sight. "This company isn't what it used to be, and Brad's death doesn't magically change him back into the nice guy he was when he started Manon Investments."

"Ms. Kent?" Marilyn turned at the sound of her name. Detective Nielsen had been finishing up a phone conversation and had yet to join Phil in the office. He slid his cell inside his suit jacket. "You're free to go. I appreciate the information you supplied to us, and I'll be following up with those individuals in question."

Grace elbowed Laurel, who in turn was watching Marilyn

closely for any hint of what Detective Nielsen could possibly be talking about. Granted, Marilyn was the eyes and ears of this company. But did she actually have some vital knowledge regarding one of the employees or clients that would implicate him or her in Brad's murder?

"Fuck," Cynthia whispered, the noise from her bracelets almost covering up her expletive. This woman, whose black hair didn't have a strand out of place or a wrinkle in her apparel, never allowed anything to phase her. "I've got to make a phone call."

Laurel and Grace would have immediately followed, but Detective Nielsen stopped them both. They could only stare after their friend as she quickly made her way through the glass doors toward the elevator bank.

"Ms. Calanthe, thank you for coming back in so soon." Detective Nielsen motioned tiredly toward the guest chairs behind them. It was a thankless job, but he was doing it nonetheless. "Please have a seat. I'll be with you as soon as I can."

Numerous things happened at once, though none of them anything Laurel wanted to deal with. She was still running on lack of sleep, regardless of the two or three hours she'd gotten at Smith's apartment. The acid she was drinking was only upsetting her stomach worse, and the tremors that had set up residence in her hands weren't diminishing the way she'd hoped.

"Laurel, may I see you out in the foyer, please?" Paul asked, though it really wasn't a question. It was obvious he'd found out about her affair with Smith. He shouldered past her through the glass doors, which happened to be where Smith stood confident-ly in a fresh change of clothes. "Now."

Forensics still wasn't allowing anyone to walk mindlessly through the offices, keeping everyone contained in the foyer.

That most likely wouldn't change until Monday morning. Laurel would have given anything to go and hide in her office until the detective asked to speak with her, but she'd been called out to face the firing squad. She just hoped that wasn't in the literal term, because the additional time it would take to close the doors on Manon Investments would allow her the months needed to secure a good paying job elsewhere.

"I'll go check on Cynthia," Grace all but whispered, resting a hand on Laurel's arm in reassurance. "Yell if you think you're going to need help."

Oh, she was already out in the middle of the ocean without a life jacket. There was no saving her from the circling sharks.

"You, too," Paul told Smith as he followed Grace to the open foyer.

Laurel was grateful to have the porcelain mug in her hand. It gave her something to grip so that she didn't try to uppercut Smith in the jaw should he say something about their relationship being long term. He'd become somewhat delusional in the last ten hours, making assumptions that weren't true.

She reluctantly walked back out the glass doors, joining the two men who had stopped near the first elevator. Grace and Cynthia were nowhere to be found, so either they went downstairs to the lobby or they continued walking toward the other side of the floor where a long hallway contained two bathrooms and a realtor's office.

"You want to tell me why I'm just now hearing that the two of you are involved from Detective Nielsen?"

"I really don't see how that is any of your business, Paul." Smith held his ground, which Laurel admired. She wasn't his biggest fan at the moment, but that didn't mean she wouldn't give praise where it was due. Unfortunately, his arrogance would only make this situation much worse. Especially considering that

Paul liked to be appeased. "What we do on our personal time is just that—personal. It didn't extend to the office."

"Paul, I apologize."

"Don't," Smith ordered, his dark gaze immediately making contact with hers. There was still an underlying anger simmering in the depth of his brown eyes, but this wasn't something that he was able to get away with just because his surname was Gallo. "Neither of us have anything to apologize for, Laurel."

"I wasn't apologizing for what we do on our personal time," Laurel corrected irritably, turning her attention back to Paul. She would have to deal with Smith at some point, but right now, she had to set her priorities straight. Paul and the business had been affected in a dire way due to Brad's death. Everyone's emotions were running on high. It was best to soothe this situation over instead of making it worse. "I'm sorry you found out about it the way you did. It was unfortunate. We meant no harm to anyone."

"The two of you are both up for the same promotion," Paul pointed out, his frustration evident. His ran a hand through his ruffled hair, which was rarely out of place. He'd had a hell of a morning, but then so had everyone else. "Do you know how this will look to the board members?"

The board members consisted of Paul, Steve Lewis, Vern Roberts, and Joshua Green. Brad also had a position at the table, but that would most likely revert to Meredith. She might have been Brad's ex-wife, but as far as any of them knew, he'd never changed his will or any of the legal paperwork that concerned Manon Investments.

"And how does our personal relationship affect the board or their decision in any way?" Smith asked, still poking a stick at a very hurt, confused, and angry lion. Couldn't he see that Paul was grieving over his friend? "It doesn't. Our work speaks for itself."

Laurel repositioned her purse on her shoulder before switching the coffee to her left hand. She wasn't sure what prompted her to do it, but she rested her hand on the sleeve of Smith's suit jacket. Something told her that he needed to know she didn't feel attacked by Paul's questioning.

"Smith, Paul is right. It is all about appearances, and that's on us." There was no way around taking full responsibility for the decisions they'd made and the reasons why. "Given what happened last night, none of this is any longer germane, though. The most important thing now is finding the person responsible and handling the outstanding business matters properly."

Paul wrapped one arm around his lower chest and used his other hand to cover his face. He began to break down, which wasn't unexpected. He and Brad had been best friends throughout college, both of them having a dream of owning their own company. They not only accomplished that vision, but they'd been successful in their endeavors as partners. They'd created a reputable hedge fund, and now it would all disintegrate into ashes as if none of it ever existed. But the most painful part of that was Paul had lost his lifelong best friend.

Smith pressed his lips together and rested a comforting hand on Paul's shoulder.

Watching this man crumble under his grief put things into perspective. She wasn't sure if it was the shock of finding Brad with his throat slit, but reality began to hit her like a two by four. Nothing mattered more in the short term than the impact of Brad's death and the loss he'd left behind for his family and friends to deal with in the aftermath.

"Ms. Calanthe?"

Paul turned away to collect himself while Smith took a step to prevent the detective from seeing the other man's grief. Her time had finally arrived to go over the accounts of last night once more, as well as any other questions the detective thought were pertinent to the case.

"We're ready for you now."

She briefly wondered who *we* consisted of, but a glance over the detective's shoulder told her that there was another officer waiting for them. Was this a good cop and bad cop scenario? She had nothing to hide, but their intimidating presence had her heart racing and her pulse accelerating.

The ding of the elevator caught everyone's attention. A tall woman stepped out into the foyer, her high heels clicking on the marble as she moved forward and rested her eyes on Smith. She allowed not one ounce of emotion to show as she took in the gathering crowd.

"It appears I'm just in time." The blonde woman shifted a designer briefcase into her left hand as she casually laid her French manicured nails on Smith's upper arm. "Is this her?"

Her obviously meant Laurel. She wasn't sure how she felt about being referred to as if she weren't standing right in front of them, but the woman's brief softening toward her and Smith's relationship came to an abrupt halt.

"Yes," Smith answered unapologetically. He murmured something to Paul before advancing forward, causing everyone else to do the same. It was obvious he'd done so in order to give Paul some time to collect himself, but Smith still wasn't off the hook for what Laurel suspected to be the truth. He'd brought in a high-end hired gun as a lawyer for their questioning without running that decision by her. "This is Meg Preston. She'll be our counsel during the questioning."

"I don't need someone representing me, Smith." Laurel couldn't stop a bit of her exhaustion slipping through her mask. She shoved the coffee cup into his hand, tired of holding it. She was out-and-out drained of any energy to get her through this upcoming interrogation, but she would persevere. "I have nothing to hide and am perfectly capable of answering a few questions."

"Not without a lawyer, you aren't. Meg is here for us both."

He was on a first name basis with his lawyer?

Laurel made the quick decision of allowing Smith this one concession. Having a lawyer present might very well reduce the time she needed to be here or in his presence. She could then go home and fall into bed with plans to sleep for the next twelve hours.

"Fine," Laurel relented, feigning a smile as she spun on her own heels to face the detective. They weren't nearly as expensive as the Jimmy Choos that Meg Preston was wearing, but they'd gotten Laurel through some tough times. "Let's do this, Ms. Preston."

CHAPTER SEVEN

"JUST HOW LONG has Laurel been in there?" Grace asked, her usual smile missing as she joined Smith in the corner of the foyer. "I would have thought she would have been done by now. What kind of lawyer did you hire?"

He'd been staring at the closed door where Detective Nielsen had escorted Laurel and Meg to conduct the interview. Smith was under no misconceptions about how these types of investigations were run, and he'd been pleased when Laurel had accepted the legal counsel he'd provided. Speaking to the authorities about anything official without representation was always a mistake. His father hadn't needed to tell him twice.

"It's been exactly forty-three minutes." Smith didn't have to look at his watch, considering he'd done so thirty seconds before Grace had walked back through the glass doors. "Did Cynthia ever get ahold of Gareth?"

"You knew?" The astonishment in Grace's tone was evident. Smith had been in this industry long enough to know that nothing important was kept secret for very long. He was, however, a bit surprised that Grace hadn't learned that vital lesson by now. It was the reason he wasn't bothered when his relationship with Laurel had been brought out into the open. The only ones who hadn't known were those few coworkers who kept to themselves or spent the majority of their time in another state or country, like Paul Slater. "And no, she hasn't been able to reach him. At least, that was the last I heard."

"Gareth and I go way back, actually," Smith divulged, his long-standing friendship with one of their biggest high net worth clients was common knowledge. "He rang me up last week, saying he'd overreacted to a situation recently. Cynthia took offense at some offhand comment he'd made. He wanted me to check on her."

"Did Gareth happen to tell you exactly what it was that he'd said, because it might land your friend behind bars."

"What are you talking about?" Smith hadn't asked Gareth for details. That wasn't how their kind of friendship worked, as it had more to do with respect than it did taking in a game on a Sunday afternoon. And as of late, his Sunday afternoons had been spent in bed with Laurel. "Are you implying Cynthia believes Gareth had something to do with Brad's murder?"

"I'm saying that it's possible that Marilyn might have taken a conversation out of context." Grace's knuckles had gone white, as if she were also worried about what Marilyn might have said during her interview. This was the problem with not being up front about situations. "If you'll excuse me, I have a phone call to make, as well."

Smith nodded, but he never took his eyes off the closed office door. He'd known Meg for years, as she was one of the many lawyers kept on retainer by his family. She was who he had chosen to see to his own personal and business dealings, though it was rare she was put in this type of position. He had no doubt that she could handle herself more than adequately, but it was her attitude toward Laurel that had him on edge at the moment.

Those two women were both very independent.

It was his belief that two type A personalities didn't mix well together, but it appeared he had nothing to worry about. Both Laurel and Meg emerged from the firm's small conference room looking more like friends than adversaries.

"Thank you, Ms. Preston." Laurel held out her arm, shaking hands with Meg as if they'd just closed the most lucrative deal of the century.

"Please, call me Meg." She pulled out a business card from the side of her briefcase, handing over her contact numbers with one of her rare smiles. "Don't hesitate to call me should you need my services again. Smith, are you ready?"

No, he wasn't ready to go into an interrogation where he would provide little information to a murder investigation he wanted nothing to do with. Brad Manon had not lived up to his name when Smith had begun working for Manon Investments. All the hype had been snuffed out the first week of his employment, especially after he'd had his first run-in with the mercurial man behind the fund.

"Laurel, I shouldn't be long." Smith closed the distance between them, wishing he could take away the dark blemishes underneath her lashes. She was running on little sleep, and he'd had a hand in that. "Please wait for me."

"Smith, I'm going home. Alone." Laurel reached up and brought her hair around so that it hung over her right shoulder. "I need some time…to sleep, to think, and to figure out what I'm going to do next. I'll call you."

Smith's first reaction was that giving Laurel some space would only allow her time to rebuild the barriers he'd managed to chip away at last night and this morning. He'd meant every word when he said that he wanted to set their future on a different path. Yet, he could see the exhaustion in her pale features.

"I'll be in touch soon, then."

Laurel rested a hand on his dress shirt as he pulled her close, pressing a soft kiss to her forehead. Their three-month affair had been rather wild and passionate, leaving them breathless after each and every evening they spent together. It wasn't something one walked away from. She'd kept him at arm's length while he'd done all he could do not to allow her to pull away from him. It was time for both of them to see their different sides.

"Get some rest." Smith finally released her, hoping he was making the right decision in letting her go home alone. "We have a lot of important decisions ahead of us, sweetheart."

Laurel snuck a glance at Meg, but neither woman commented on his declaration. It was more than apparent that Nielsen had overheard them as well, but again, Smith wasn't concerned about anyone's opinion regarding his personal life, not even the one remaining partner. Smith continued to monitor Laurel's progress as she walked through the glass door. She didn't have long to wait after pressing the elevator button and soon disappeared behind the sliding door.

"Shall we?" Meg patiently waited for Smith to finally enter the office where Detective Nielsen was waiting for them on one side of the conference table. The other detective was standing near a window overlooking South Marquette Avenue. He wasn't someone Smith recognized, which was unusual seeing as the Gallos often hosted a charity dinner for local law enforcement agencies. "Detective, we're ready when you are."

"Smith, let's forgo the formalities, shall we?" Fred Nielsen held back his tie as he took a seat behind the mostly empty table. This office was reserved for clients who had need for privacy, allowing them easy access to a phone, desk, and computer. "You previously stated that you were with Ms. Calanthe until after midnight. The coroner is placing Brad Manon's death around ten o'clock last night. I'll get right to the point. Do you know of anyone who would want to see Brad Manon dead for any reason at all?"

"Look, Manon wasn't the easiest man to get along with," Smith began, joining Fred in having a seat. Meg took the second guest chair, listening intently and ensuring that the questions asked and responses given were answered with his best interest in mind. "Manon had his share of enemies just as anyone in this business has. There were quite a lot of individuals who were envious of his current success, but he made it his business to hire the best and the brightest. He had a good team behind him, which would have guaranteed his future success."

"Speaking of his team, was there anyone in the office behaving oddly or maybe even vocal about their dislike for Manon?"

"I would take whatever Marilyn says with a grain of salt," Smith advised, crossing his leg as he settled in for the duration. "The trading desk consists of Steve Lewis and Joshua Green. Steve tends to be a little on the serious side, whereas Josh is the one who's constantly mixing the sugar with salt. He likes to get a reaction. They're very vocal about their likes and dislikes, and that includes attitudes about people around this place. But neither one of them has the ability to cut a man's throat from ear to ear and watch him bleed out. And before you ask about the rumors of Manon being in debt, I honestly haven't the slightest clue about his personal financial status."

"What about Slater?" The other detective, who had been silent up to this point, finally turned his attention to those in the room. Smith took an immediate dislike to the man. "It's our understanding that Paul wanted to bring in another managing partner."

"I'm sorry," Smith countered, meeting the man's gaze without hesitation. It was also Smith's way of delaying his response. He had no idea that Paul was thinking of doing something so drastic. "And who might you be?"

"I'm the detective who—"

"My partner," Fred cut in, shooting his colleague a warning glance. "Smith, this is Detective Richard Mancini. He just transferred in from New York. He hasn't been completely read in."

Fred left out that because Mancini wasn't from around here, he didn't know all the movers and shakers, but that had been his intention. Smith honestly didn't care about that. It was rare he used his surname to take advantage of anything, discounting yesterday when he'd done so in order to reach Laurel.

For her, pride could take a back seat.

Smith's problem with Mancini was that he was too brash and had no time for anyone who couldn't help him solve a case. At least, that's the first impression Smith had gotten when he'd walked into the room.

"Well, Detective Mancini, let me set the record straight for you." Smith held up his hand when Meg began to balk. Yes, it was her job to protect him. Yes, it was the reason she was kept on retainer by the Gallos. But he also understood that the police were at a loss as to why Manon was killed, and that any information at this point could be relevant. "I wasn't aware of Paul bringing on another managing partner. Paul hasn't been in the office much over the last few months nor did he confide in me."

"And is that unusual?"

"Which? Him not confiding in me or the fact that he hadn't bothered to come to the office very often? No to both," Smith replied, giving a truthful observation on the behavior he'd seen during his employment here. "Paul is great at bringing in the money. He's usually out with clients ninety percent of the time, whether on the golf course, having lunch, or just paying them a visit in Barbados. Brad was the one responsible for turning a profit on the money Paul had brought into the fund."

"So it's reasonable to say that you would benefit professionally by Manon's death, considering you'd like to step into his shoes." Detective Mancini went straight in for the kill, but his aim was a little off given that he wasn't in possession of all the facts. Smith wasn't caught unaware, having seen where this conversation was headed the moment the man opened his mouth. "Isn't that right?"

"Meg?" Smith stood, bringing this particular questioning session to an end. He smoothed his tie before buttoning his suit jacket, not worried when Mancini stepped forward to block his exit. Better men than him had tried and failed to intimidate Smith by use of sheer will. "I'll let you take over from here. Detective Mancini, it was…well, whatever it was."

Smith never broke eye contact, waiting patiently for the detective to step aside. The man eventually rubbed his tongue across his lower lip as if he wanted to say something in protest, but he eventually gave in to the inevitable loss.

"Gentleman, my client came here in good faith, willing to answer any of your questions you may…"

Smith closed the door behind him with full confidence Meg would handle what had turned out to be a clusterfuck. He'd kept his private dealings just that…private. No phone calls were made at the office, no public meetings had taken place here in the city, and he honestly never had any intention of poaching from Manon Investments' client list.

In hindsight, there was no possible way for Detective Mancini to have known of Smith's plans regarding his intentions to open his own hedge fund unless Laurel let it slip during her time in that office. Yet Meg had been with her the entire time, ruling out that slim possibility due to her lack of objection to the detective's misplaced accusation.

Had Laurel mentioned his plans to Grace? Maybe Cynthia? And they, in turn, said something during their time with the detectives?

It was possible, but highly unlikely.

Smith didn't like the way this day was unfolding. Last night, Brad Manon had been killed and everyone had assumed it was because of the mountain of debt he'd found himself buried under. That had quickly spiraled to finger pointing and conspiracies.

Smith had lived the majority of his life being targeted because of his last name. The most vital question on the forefront now changed the course of this investigation.

Had Manon been murdered due to his own poor choices or was his death nothing more than a means to an end to bring Smith Gallo down?

CHAPTER EIGHT

L AUREL PRIED HER eyes open and stared into the abyss of darkness.

She tried to think of absolutely nothing, but her mind wouldn't cooperate. Her thoughts were racing, and nothing could slow them down. She turned over under the warm sheets and nestled deeper into her pillow in an attempt to clear her mind.

Thud. Thud. Thud.

Laurel sat straight up in bed, her gaze going directly to the bedside table. The alarm clock read that is was going on eight-thirty at night. She'd been lying here all day with little to show for her efforts.

She grabbed her phone off the charger before swinging her legs over the side of the bed. Only one of her slippers was where she'd left it, so she finally turned on the light to see if the other one had been kicked underneath the bed.

It was nowhere to be found.

She decided slippers and her bed were much like socks and the dryer.

More heavy knocking came at the door.

"Damn it," Laurel muttered, quickly making her way through the bedroom and out into the living room. She stubbed her toe on the side table up against the wall, the very reason she'd gotten those damn slippers to begin with. The pain was momentarily blinding, as it always was. She was relatively sure her little toe had been broken twenty-three million times in the years she'd lived here, but she'd been too embarrassed to go and get x-rays.

"I'm coming! Hold on!"

Laurel hopped the rest of the way, sparing one glance at the display on her phone. Sure enough, Grace and Cynthia both had texted her numerous times throughout the day. There were also quite a few messages from Smith, but she wasn't ready to deal with that emotional baggage quite yet. She finally reached her small foyer, flipping the deadbolt and swinging open the door while standing on one foot.

"I'm so sorry. I didn't hear the—"

Laurel fought the urge to slam the door in Smith's face. He was still wearing the same suit he'd changed into earlier this morning, his shave still fresh, and not a strand of his thick hair out of place. He looked just as good as if he'd gotten dressed an hour ago.

Unlike her.

She was a wreck.

Laurel was wearing what she always wore to bed, which was a pair of black running shorts, a pink t-shirt that had a hole in the shoulder due to wear, and the scrunchy that held her hair up in what was sure to look like she'd been in a hurricane. She could even see the flyaway wisps standing out from the side of her head. It was just the impressions she wanted to make.

"What the hell are you doing here?"

The words she'd been thinking in her head came tumbling out of her mouth, but she decided she wasn't going to apologize. There had been rules in place for a reason. Their conversation from earlier did *not* change the one where she went to his place if she wanted companionship, not the reverse. Besides, her little toe was still throbbing. She wasn't in the mood to be nice to anyone.

"Are you hurt?" Smith's eyes had slowly grazed over her entire body, not leaving an inch unseen, until his concerned gaze landed on her pink toe. "What happened?"

"Smith, what are you doing here?" Laurel had no choice but to hop back when he crossed the threshold. "And how did you even know where I live?"

Laurel was losing control of things again, just when she thought she'd gotten herself sorted. Granted, being away from Smith's intimidating presence might have had something to do with the illusion of control. She had a clear head when he wasn't around. Hence, why it was in both their best interests that he left forthwith.

"Here." Smith leaned down and scooped her up into his arms before she could stop him. He used the bottom of his dress shoe to close the door behind him. "Let's see what damage you've caused."

"Would you please put me down? I stubbed my toe, that's all. I didn't break my leg."

Laurel cringed when she saw the sight of her kitchen, wishing she'd turned the overhead light off when she'd gone to bed. There were still dishes in the sink, an old cup of coffee on the counter from yesterday morning, and a basket of dirty clothes near the closet doors that hid her washer and dryer. This was an affordable one-bedroom apartment that she could manage while still paying on her student loans, and she didn't need Mister Money Bucks scrutinizing her living arrangements.

"Did you break it? It's beginning to swell." Smith set her on the counter, which happened to be ice cold. She couldn't help but inhale sharply when the back of her thighs made contact with the laminate. "Let me take a closer look."

The faint scent of Smith's expensive cologne was a temptation she could have done without, along with the warmth of his strong hands, which now traveled down her left leg until he'd set her foot against his rock-hard abs. She closed her eyes and did her best to picture him a hundred pounds heavier with a receding hairline.

No luck.

"Ouch!" The comical vision she'd conjured up faded the moment he tried to wiggle her toe. Laurel would have yanked her foot away had he not had a good hold on her ankle. "Watch it, Harvard boy! That hurt."

"It's not broken, but that's a hell of a stubbed toe." Smith carefully released her leg so that he could walk over to the refrigerator. She wanted to cry out to him that she didn't need any ice, but it was too late. "Um, what is that?"

"What is what?" Laurel hopped off the counter, leaving her phone behind. She quickly hobbled over to where he had the bottom drawer of the freezer open while staring at the contents in somewhat shock. She didn't blame him for the bewildered look. "Oh, that. It's nothing."

Laurel shoved the drawer closed with her good foot, which happened to be the one with a slipper on it. She would have been somewhat embarrassed by her state of dress had another dose of anger not shot through her bloodstream.

"Smith, I'm going to ask you one last time," Laurel said, making her intentions known. "What. Are. You. Doing. Here?"

"Pretending like nothing has changed between us gets us nowhere."

Smith was apparently letting her off the hook about what was in her freezer, but he was sailing into uncharted territory. At least, according to her calculations.

"Look around you, Smith." Laurel so didn't want to have this conversation, especially now that her entire life was leaking water through holes that were too big to plug with her big toe. She leaned back against the refrigerator, still mentally exhausted. The eight hours of fitful sleep she'd gotten had done nothing to shake her fatigue. Her barriers had been chipped away, and she honestly didn't have the strength to reconstruct them. "Seriously, look around this place and tell me that what we have has a chance of lasting a New York minute? I don't do charity balls or run in the same social circle as your royal court. I still have student loans, while making sure my mom has enough grocery money to eat for the month. We're both workaholics. We'd never see one another. You're about to open your own hedge fund somewhere in the city. I'm most likely going to end up in New York panhandling while I look for a position at one of the investment banks. It won't work, Smith."

"Do you want to make it work? Or are you quitting?"

It was such a simple question, yet it held so many land mines that she was almost afraid to breathe. Smith took a step forward. He tucked some of those flyaway strands behind her ear in a gentle manner he rarely exhibited. It was when he tilted her face up so that she caught the look of hope flare in his dark eyes that she answered him honestly.

"Yes, but—"

Smith kissed her, once again with a gentleness that surprised her. It wasn't the all-consuming beginning of another late evening tryst that they usually engaged in on the weekdays. No, this was the start of something that absolutely terrified the shit out of her.

His tongue gently caressed her bottom lip until she allowed him to play with hers. He tasted of whiskey and mint, a heady combination. She would have asked where he'd come from this late at night, but her body was responding with its inherent need for security. Even the throbbing in her little toe somewhat subsided, taking up residence someplace else in her mindset. Conversation could definitely wait until later, when she was sure regret would rear its ugly head.

"That's the only answer that matters to me." Smith lifted her back up into his arms, causing her one slipper to fall to the floor. One slipper really wasn't much good anyway. He walked out of the kitchen and through her small living room, which actually happened to look good since she hadn't been home much. There were only two other rooms in the apartment; her bathroom and bedroom. Both doors were side by side and it was obvious which was which. "Please tell me that you—"

Knock. Knock. Knock.

"Weren't expecting company?"

"No, I wasn't. But then you showed up." Laurel appreciated that Smith carefully set her back on her feet, allowing her to cross the tile with some dignity. This time, she did utilize the peephole. Her stomach sank as recognition dawned. "Um, Smith? You might want to give Meg a call."

Laurel wasn't dressed to receive a visit from the two detectives she'd spoken to earlier, but it wasn't like she could keep them waiting out in the hallway while she got dressed. She would have loved to have a bit of time to calm her racing heart, given that she'd been about to engage in extracurricular activities. It wasn't easy to go from arousal to putting on a makeshift attempt at a professional air.

She wrapped her trembling hand around the doorknob, not looking back to see if Smith was following her advice. It wasn't like they were here to arrest anyone, given that neither she nor Smith had done anything wrong. And even if that were the case, extremely unlikely as that may be, they were still allowed one phone call before processing. She'd seen enough television shows to know that bit of information.

"Detectives," Laurel greeted cautiously while throwing them a look of apology. "Please, join the party."

"What can we do for you?" Smith asked, getting right to the point. He remained where he was on the edge of the living room carpet. "As you can imagine, Laurel has had a rough twenty-four hours."

"We have a couple of follow-up questions." Detective Nielsen quietly closed the door behind them once Laurel took a few steps back. The gravity of his inquiry was etched in the lines around his eyes. "We'd also like—"

"Please," Laurel interrupted, not comfortable with another interview while dressed like she was a teenager at a sleepover. "Give me a moment to get dressed, and I'll be right with you. Smith, would you please make everyone some coffee or offer them something to drink?"

She didn't wait for Smith to acknowledge her request. He wanted to be a part of her life. Well, she wasn't the most domestic type of woman he could have found. It was better that he discovered that sooner rather than later.

It took her less than five minutes to change into decent clothes, brush her teeth, and draw a brush through her tangled bird's nest. She grabbed a light shade of lipstick, spreading a thin layer on her lips to give her some form of color. There were no sounds of gunshots, raised voices, or Smith calling out for her to phone Meg, which meant the men were keeping things civilized. The relative quietness also told her that no imminent arrests were on the horizon.

"So," Laurel said, breezing into the kitchen wearing a pair of jeans and a red buttoned-down blouse. The outfit gave her the air of confidence, but comfort was her intent. At least, that's how she hoped they viewed her attitude. "What are these questions that you have for me, detectives?"

She might have made assumptions a little too soon, because Smith appeared ready to throw the men out on their collective asses. That wouldn't have gone over well, and the consequences would have been a never-ending legal battle where Meg was paid enough to afford another pair of those gorgeous designer high heels. She also noted that no one was drinking any coffee.

"We would actually prefer to speak with you alone, Ms. Calanthe."

It didn't take a genius to figure out that specific appeal was the one that had riled Smith. She couldn't blame him, either. A flash of Brad's unfocused eyes flickered in her mind, breaking her concentration. She'd done her best not to think about the horror of what she'd witnessed, but nothing seemed to eradicate the disturbing images that floated back to the surface.

She pulled out a chair and joined Detective Nielsen at the table. Smith remained standing, his arms crossed as he leaned back against the kitchen counter. As for Detective Mancini, he remained standing with his gaze focused solely on Smith.

"Since you didn't call me down to the station nor notify my attorney, I can assume this isn't an official interview." Laurel debated on whether or not Meg should be present, but she wanted to hear what direction this line of questioning was headed before she made that call. "What is it that you're—"

"You do realize that Laurel is being represented by Meg Preston. Questioning her without her attorney present is suspect at best. She also reserves the right to end this visit at any time."

Laurel wasn't surprised that Smith didn't want her to say anything without representation. But she also wanted to help these detectives in any way that she could, provided that they kept an open mind about who could be responsible. She'd worked with almost every employee at the firm for many, many years. She couldn't imagine any of them committing murder, let alone in a manner so hideous as this.

"We understand that you wouldn't want your girlfriend here to say something that could incriminate you, but the world doesn't revolve around you, Mr. Gallo." Detective Mancini had been a little rough around the edges when he'd questioned her, but his obvious dislike for Smith made her uncomfortable. Laurel immediately sought out Detective Nielsen's gaze, silently telling him that was the wrong tact to take under the circumstances. "This has to do with Cynthia Ellsworth and her relationship with one of your high net worth individuals."

"You mean Gareth Nicollet?"

"Yes," Detective Nielsen replied, taking over the conversation. It didn't help divert Detective Mancini's focus on what he perceived as a connection to the murder. She'd been with Smith at the time Brad had been attacked in his office. There was no reason for that type of hostility. "You see, we have it on good authority that Gareth Nicollet threatened Mr. Manon's life not one week ago."

"You happen to be good friends with the same Mr. Nicollet, isn't that right?"

"Mancini, why don't you go and pull the car around?" Detective Nielsen stood from the table, not giving the other man the ability to refuse. "I'll finish up here."

At first, Laurel wasn't so sure that Detective Mancini would do as Nielsen suggested. Technically, it wasn't a suggestion. She was honestly surprised when the man turned on the heel of his well-worn dress shoe and made his way to her front door. No one spoke until after the latch caught, signaling he'd finally vacated the apartment.

"Fred, you want to tell me what his problem is?" Smith asked, not the type of man to become someone else's punching bag. "This seems to be some personal beef he's got, but I'm at a loss here. I've had my fill of insults and innuendos. My next step won't be talking to you about your partner's behavior."

"Mancini is new and out to prove to the brass that he won't favor anyone based on their last name or checking account." Detective Nielsen seemed to debate on whether or not to share more information. He chose wisely. "He also had a run-in with your father earlier regarding Sebastian."

It was rare that Smith and Laurel discussed family during the times they were together, but she was aware that Sebastian and Solomon were his brothers. Sebastian was the youngest, having just graduated college and was supposed to be studying for the bar. She'd gotten that information from a brief phone call that Smith had with his father one evening when they were together.

"What did Sebastian do this time?"

There was a disappointment in Smith's tone that was unrecognizable. She resisted the urge to reach out to comfort him, but then realized she didn't have to do that anymore...not if they were truly serious about going public with their relationship.

Were they going public?

Was now the right time for anything?

Laurel instinctively pushed back the chair and took the three steps to where Smith was still leaning against the counter. She joined him, slipping her fingers underneath his crossed arms. Her heart warmed when his hand covered hers in appreciation.

"He got into a fight over at First Ave. Listen, I'm not here to discuss your brother. I'm here because of the threat Gareth Nicollet made on Brad Manon's life. I need answers."

First Avenue was a famous hotspot in the city, and one that Laurel frequented often with her friends. She'd seen the famous younger Gallo there a time or two. He'd yet to grow up, and he certainly didn't handle his liquor very well.

As for Gareth, he was a true philanthropist. He was the head of multiple charities and traveled the world extensively, spreading the wealth of his family in strategic locations. His time, effort, and contributions to veterans, the homeless, and those in need were beyond astounding.

"Gareth is a passionate man about many things," Smith conceded, declining to mention the fact that Detective Mancini had been most likely forced to drop charges against Sebastian. "If he said anything of the sort, it was most likely taken out of context."

"I agree." Laurel recalled Cynthia having an argument with Gareth over their relationship. They dated occasionally on the down low, but she recalled Cynthia saying she'd had a run-in with Brad regarding the fact that she was technically the compliance officer dating a client. She'd mentioned it to Gareth, who'd stopped by the office while doing business in the city. It was rare, but he'd done it just the same. His reaction to Brad's suggestion hadn't gone over so well, but Gareth hadn't meant he would literally kill Brad. "Gareth is a great guy. Ask anyone. I recall that specific conversation, and it was a meaningless turn of a phrase."

Marilyn, no doubt, had filled both of the detectives' heads with information that she'd dramatized.

"And Cynthia Ellsworth?" The reason for Detective Nielsen's visit had finally dawned, and Laurel didn't appreciate that the police were focusing on her friends or those colleagues she'd worked with over the years. "What about her? Do you think she's capable of murdering Brad Manon?"

CHAPTER NINE

SMITH TOSSED THE empty Chinese containers into Laurel's trashcan she kept under the sink. It never ceased to amaze him how much food they could pack into one of those little containers. The place two blocks over had the most incredible spring rolls. Apparently, Laurel was a regular and craved the shrimp fried rice as opposed to the regular white that came with nearly every entrée.

Smith had originally come over to her apartment to ask if she'd mentioned anything to either detective regarding his new business venture, but things had quickly gone down another path the second she'd opened the door wearing short shorts and a nearly see-through t-shirt that left nothing to the imagination. Not that his imagination was very limited. He knew her body better than any woman he'd ever been with.

She had looked sexy as hell, instantly derailing the primary reason of his visit.

The frozen breastmilk in her freezer had put a speedbump in his plans to ice her toe before carrying her into the bedroom for mouth to mouth, should she have a need for it. The one thing he should be grateful for was that her necessity to change the subject had clarified where both of them stood in this relationship.

As for her coming to stand next to him when he was talking about his younger brother, well, that told him she was open to more than a quick fuck after a long workday.

"I mean, if someone we work with did kill Brad, who do you think could do something so inhumane as to slit Brad's throat so gruesomely?" Laurel asked, putting the leftover wonton soup in the refrigerator. They'd spent most of the meal discussing this very topic, but he couldn't prevent his gaze from dropping to the freezer drawer once again. "If I had to pick, I would say Steve. You know, I immediately feel guilty for even thinking that. And I would never, ever say anything to the police along those lines. I'm just glad we put to rest the fact that Cynthia could never hurt anyone, let alone brutally murder someone. Besides, she was at a business dinner until ten o'clock that night. She even joined the hangers-on for cocktails afterward."

"Laurel, why is there frozen breastmilk in your freezer? I'm coming up empty trying to imagine why. Please tell me that you don't use it for coffee creamer."

"Oh, that." Laurel brushed off the unusual item with a wave of her hand. She walked past him and picked up both of their wine glasses, which he'd topped off so that he could toss the bottle into the recycling bin next to the trash. "That's for the twins. Don't worry. They're at their father's house this week-end."

There was rarely a time when Smith was taken by surprise. Those moments were even fewer where he couldn't form a string of words to form a retort.

This was one of those times.

"I'm kidding, Harvard boy. You can breathe again." Laurel flashed a smile over her shoulder. "One of my neighbors *does* have twins, but she doesn't have enough room in her freezer to store a supply of additional bags. And seeing as Auntie Laurel babysits now and then, it seemed practical that I store the overflow allotment here."

Smith remained where he was at the kitchen sink, letting her walk into the living room while he wrapped his mind around the image of her holding an infant.

Who was he kidding?

The vision itself was almost enough to satisfy what he needed to get over the shock value of her Machiavellian jest.

Her sense of humor was oddly twisted.

Laurel never mentioned children before, none of her friends that he knew of had children, and she radiated the fact that she was highly focused on her career. The partnership they were both previously competing for had been all she could focus on for the last three months. This was a side of her that he never knew existed, but a sense of fulfillment washed over him at the thought of what their future could hold with the two of them side by side with an estate in Sands Point.

The thing of it was that he'd never planned on taking her partnership from her in the first place. Regardless of how he tried to communicate that now, it came out sounding like sour grapes. There had been no doubt that had he dropped out early on in the running someone else would have entered the picture.

Nature abhors a vacuum.

Her chances might have been diminished, though.

He hadn't been able do that to her.

Hell, Phil Colbert had chosen two technology stocks that had grown by twenty percent between the two of them in the last few months. Had he chosen to profess any of this aloud, she would have taken offense, and rightly so.

It wasn't that he didn't think she'd earned a spot at that table, but more often than not there were ethereal variables which came into play. Laurel deserved that partnership, she'd worked hard for that partnership, and now it was likely gone forever given what would most likely happen to the company—

full divesture of funds to established firms and dissolution of the partnership.

It wasn't like people lived forever in the financial world. Most investors had an opportunity to adjust to new partners or key players growing into their positions over time, maintaining continuity within an institution.

Brad had been the whole show with nobody in the wings.

"Are you joining me or what?" Laurel called out from the living room. "I can't promise not to drink your wine if you dally."

Smith smiled, liking this casual side of Laurel that she'd always shielded from him. He'd removed his jacket earlier, rolling up his sleeves so that he could eat without staining the cuffs. He'd loosened his tie as well, having no intention of leaving tonight. It was going to be interesting to see what her reaction would be to his proposal of spending the night at her place for once.

"Boys, girls, or one of each?" Smith pulled his tie from around his neck in one smooth stroke and promptly tossed it onto the coffee table, noticing that she was still holding his wineglass. She was curled up on the couch, her left toe free from her weight. It was still slightly pink, but she was no longer favoring it when she walked. "And how many months?"

"Why are you even remotely interested?" Laurel asked, skepticism written across her beautiful features.

Her hair was still down, cascading around her shoulders and catching the light in such a way that her highlights shimmered with a golden hue. She finally offered him his glass when he claimed the cushion next to her.

"What kind of question is that? Are you questing my intentions?"

"You're...I don't know. You just don't strike me as the

family type."

"I'm a damn fine uncle to a niece and nephew," Smith shared, reaching for her legs to draw them over his lap. He made sure to only massage her good foot. By the way she parted her lips and closed her eyes, he'd made the right choice. "I happen to love kids."

"You keep doing that, and I'll give you as many as you'd like," Laurel muttered, clearly joking as she had been before. But she had no idea how appealing that thought was to him. He took a sip of the red merlot she'd had on hand to prevent himself from saying something that would give her hesitation. He even took his time savoring the earthy flavor of the grapes. "You have to admit that you being here at my place is off. It feels weird."

"What's so off about it?" Smith rested his left arm across the back of the couch, resting his wineglass on top of the cushion. She'd sunk into the decorative pillow behind her, her hair fanning itself around her like a halo. "Me rubbing your foot? I've done that and much more, little minx."

Laurel's light laugh echoed around the comfortable room. Her décor was done in earth tones, but she also had splashes of vibrant colors strategically placed around the room. It was different from his own apartment, which was very sterile in comparison. He hadn't personally chosen any of the designs. He had a decorator apply the generic yet high-end bachelor package without depending on any particular school of design. Laurel's touches said a hell of a lot more about her than his package plan said about him.

"Having a conversation other than work or…"

"Sex?" Smith flashed her a smile. "Sorry, great sex."

"You don't see any issues standing in the way of moving our relationship forward, do you?"

"And why would I?" Now this was a topic that he could

appreciate. "I knew from the moment I walked into your office to introduce myself that there was something between us. It was only natural to see it through to its inevitable conclusion."

"Sexual attraction doesn't mean anything other than a couple might enjoy a good time in bed." Laurel wasn't quite as relaxed as her body language led him to believe. Her green eyes were watching him very closely, gauging his reaction to her probes. "What makes you think there's more to this than that?"

"And what makes people consider that sex is just copulating?" Smith slowly drew a finger down the underside of her foot. Her toes curled instinctively, the red nails arching due to the stimulating sensation. "What makes you think that what we have is just sex without the obvious intimacy?"

"I honestly don't know what kind of intimacy we have," Laurel whispered, catching on rather quickly that he'd rather show her than tell her. She took another healthy sip of her wine. "We live completely separate lives. Much of which you've never questioned before, Smith. It's rare that our paths cross in everyday life for anything other than *great sex*."

"It doesn't have to be that way. You just need to invest yourself." Smith leaned forward and set his wineglass on the coffee table. He then unbuttoned her jeans, slowly sliding the zipper down its golden track. "Is there something stopping you from attending a charity ball with me? I've seen you at other social events. You have excellent taste in clothing and apparently have an insatiable shoe fetish."

"There's nothing like buying a brand-new pair of designer heels," Laurel said somewhat breathlessly. She was holding her wineglass out away from herself so that she didn't spill any as he slid the denim over her heart-shaped ass. "As a matter of fact, I recall you admiring those red Valentino Garavani heels I got for seventy percent off at Saks. It was a milestone victory of mine."

"I like them very much." Smith remembered the exact evening he'd had her keep them on, along with her black lace garter belt and matching seamed stockings. Of course, that was all she had left on while they'd had sex on his granite-topped kitchen island. This was the perfect time to let her know they were having dinner with his family. "You can wear them tomorrow evening when we have dinner with my parents."

Smith apparently hadn't thought through her extreme reaction to such a statement. After all, they'd just agreed to see this relationship past the point in which they merely used each other to scratch an itch. Did she truly believe that it wouldn't eventually involve meeting his family?

Laurel jolted straight up from the couch, giving him time to reach for the wineglass before the red contents spilled all over her cream carpet. He relieved her of the delicate stemmed glassware. She was shaking her head vigorously in response to his invitation.

"Absolutely not." Laurel began to shift her weight rapidly from side to side so that she could pull up her jeans. "I am not—"

"I didn't realize that you had some type of grudge against my parents."

"What?" Laurel managed to get the waist of her jeans back in place, but his theory prevented her from finishing the job. Lines of confusion appeared on her forehead as she began to protest. *Good.* That had been his intention all along. "I don't—"

"It's fine. Truly. I'll inform them that you don't want to meet them and—"

"You're playing me, Smith," Laurel said angrily, sweeping her hair to the side. He couldn't help but smirk at her tell. "See. There. That smile. You can't guilt me into having dinner with your mother and father."

"Why not? It's just a meal. Is there a reason I can't take the woman I'm serious about to a family function? Is there a waiting period or some kind of prerequisite I'm unaware of?"

Smith leaned over her legs to set her wineglass next to his, doing his best not to show he'd gambled and underestimated her reaction. He'd made a left turn, when it would have been better to take a right. He'd allowed it to become too intimate too quickly. It was obvious she was still wary about where they were headed, so he rectified his error in judgement.

"Like I said, it's okay. I'll let them know you'd rather not attend dinner tomorrow night. It's a shame, though. I have no doubt my father has garnered more inside information regarding the investigation into Brad's murder." Smith took her foot into both hands, using his fingers to dig into her arch to try and relax her against the stress building in her shoulders while she contemplated meeting his parents as someone special in his life. "I might not appreciate the way he does business outside of the courtroom, but he is effective at using our surname to his advantage."

"I hate you right now."

"You love me." Smith continued to concentrate on the light massage he was giving her, understanding full well the implications of his reply. He let the weight of his words settle over her before he made light of the situation. "But it's all fine. I'll go myself, ward off the questions that I'm sure will be asked about you and your motives, and then play in the den with my niece and nephew to avoid the inevitable repercussions."

"Hide in the den," Laurel muttered with a shake of her head. She fell back against her pillow in defeat. "Only rich people say *in the den*. But fine. I'll go. I'm not wearing those heels or the stockings, for that matter."

"Why not?" Smith wiggled his eyebrows, showing her that

he did have a lighter side, despite what she may think. "Oh, you don't want to think about the great sex we had while we're—"

Laurel cut off his words when she reared back up and straddled him. Her kiss prevented any more conversation about his family. It always astonished him how the air around them instantly electrified with a simple touch. She began unfastening his dress shirt and tugging the hem from his waistband.

"You talk too much," Laurel whispered seductively, her soft lips trailing over his jawline and down his neck. He leaned forward enough to remove his dress shirt and toss it to the floor. "Let's see what I can do about that."

Smith wasn't about to argue as she gradually removed herself from the couch, only to then carefully kneel on the carpet and position herself directly between his legs.

His cock hardened at the thought of what was to come.

"I want you naked when you suck me off," Smith ordered with a heavy tone, unable to prevent his arousal from dripping off his words. He grabbed her wrist to stop her from reaching for his belt. "Get undressed, little minx."

In no time, both of them were naked and back in position. The smooth slide of her hands traveling up his thighs and toward his rock hard cock had him inhaling sharply. She wrapped her fingers around his shaft, slowly stroking him while she appeared mesmerized by the drop of pre-cum he'd emitted from the tip.

"Laurel, you have five minutes before I turn you over the arm of this couch and fuck you until you're screaming my name and begging for another just like the first."

The slow spread of her smile let him know just how much she liked that vision. One of her favorite positions was being taken from behind, and he had to say that there was definitely appeal in that particular arrangement. He was able to sink deeper into her, connecting them in an entirely different way.

"Then I best get going on those five minutes," Laurel said teasingly with another pump of her hand. She even drew her thumb over his tip, drawing out a low moan of satisfaction from his chest. "Three, two, one…"

Laurel's warm lips closed over his cock, but the warmth was nothing compared to the heat of her tongue. She stroked across his opening before taking more of him in her mouth. She pulled back, using the palm of her hand to smear what wetness she'd left behind. Again, she sucked him back in, but this time to the back of her throat.

He wanted nothing more than to lean his head back against the cushion, but he wouldn't miss the beautiful sight before him for all the money in the world.

Her chestnut locks had fallen off her shoulders, fanning out over his thighs. A flush had settled over her cheekbones while her lashes rested against her skin as she savored his taste. There was nothing quite as arousing than the image of a woman pleasuring a man.

Laurel's tongue glided over the underside of his cock, but her hair had hidden her face when she'd tilted her head to the side. It gave him the perfect opportunity to tangle his fingers in her hair, pulling ever so slightly so that he could see her expression when he told her what he'd really like her to do with her free hand.

"Spread your knees, Laurel. Spread them so that you can stroke your clit. I want you ready for when I bend you over."

Laurel's green eyes darkened to almost black and her nostrils flared as she breathed in sharply. The stronger tug on his cock by the suction of her mouth told him she liked the idea, but it wasn't until her eyes fluttered closed again at her own pleasure that he came very close to coming in her mouth.

"That's right," Smith murmured, doing his best to restrain himself. He'd promised her five minutes, and he never went back on his word. "Rub yourself even harder. Are you completely drenched?"

Another guttural groan vibrated his cock to the point where he involuntarily tightened his fingers in her hair. That only seemed to fuel her desire for more, because she tightened the fingers of her left hand at the bottom of his shaft. It both helped and hurt him in his attempt to prevent his release.

Smith had no choice but to release his hold on her hair, quickly reaching inside one of the back pockets of his slacks to withdraw a condom from his wallet. Laurel didn't even seem to notice as she continued to suck him while pleasuring herself simultaneously.

"Don't you come, little minx," Smith warned, gritting his teeth against the inevitable orgasm. He refused to allow his body the pleasure until he was balls deep inside of her. He ripped open the foil with his teeth and removed the small disc. "Stop."

Laurel tossed her hair back when she did as he directed, knowing full well that relief was minutes away.

"Slide your middle finger inside of yourself," Smith muttered, never taking his eyes off her face as he rolled the latex over his cock. Even his own touch was almost too much, but he finally secured the condom at the base of his shaft. He knew the exact moment she entered herself, for her lips parted and her eyes glazed over in pleasure. "Now it's my turn."

Smith made quick the decision that the arm of the couch just wasn't good enough. He had her positioned with her knees facing the back of the cushions, giving him just the right amount of leverage where he claimed her in one thrust.

Laurel cried out his name before resting her cheek against her inner arm. Smith continued to drive himself into her the way they both relished, not giving time for either one of them to catch their breaths. It wasn't until he was on the verge of that impending release that he reached around, taking up where she'd left off.

She was so wet that he had no trouble gathering her juices and rubbing her clit until her fingers dug into the cushion.

"That's right, little minx," Smith whispered the encouragement into her ear. "Come for me."

The tightness of his sac became even stronger as he exploded, his seed filling the condom until he had nothing more left to give. The contractions of her sheath were still pulsating as he slowly pulled out of her, drawing her down onto the couch with him so that he could hold her until they got their bearings.

"You never disappoint, Harvard boy," Laurel murmured somewhat breathlessly, her eyes already closed as she nestled deeper into his chest. The rest of her words came out in a mumble, but he was smiling by the end of her tirade. "Fine. I'll go with you to your family dinner, but I'm not wearing those damned shoes."

CHAPTER TEN

" I CALLED YOU in hopes that you could talk some sense into me," Laurel said harshly into the phone while staring at herself in the mirror of Smith's bathroom. "Grace, you need to call me back in five minutes and say you have an emergency you need my help with."

Laurel had gotten dressed at her apartment, though that was a bit of an understatement. It had taken her trying on five different outfits before settling on a pair of black dress pants and a cream silk blouse that had bell sleeves. She'd also worn black flats out of spite. She'd now changed her mind about this whole bleeding mess. She needed to hit the back door running.

Her makeup was flawless, giving her the luxury of being stressed about the upcoming dinner without anyone the wiser. Lipstick and eyeliner were wonderful weapons. Makeup was better camouflage than the troops had in combat.

Other than that?

She was a complete mental wreck.

What had she been thinking? Who the hell thought having dinner with Smith's family had been a good idea? She'd given a little ground in the relationship department, but then the whole meeting the family thing flew up in her face. Wasn't there supposed to be a timeline for these kinds of things? Didn't that garner her some contractual amount of time to get used to being the eye candy on Smith Gallo's arm?

"You let him sleep over at your place, Laurel," Grace said wryly, not telling Laurel something she didn't already know. "Common sense went out the window last night, so you're a little late on that front. Wait. You're not pregnant, are you?"

"No, I'm not with child. Jesus Christ! I'm going to hyperventilate now. I think my chest might explode." Laurel bent at the waist, resting her forearms on the edge of the countertop. She tried to even out her breathing so she wouldn't pass out. "His parents are going to hate me. They'll think I'm after the money, his trust fund, or whatever those Ivy League bean counters call their ill-gotten fortunes."

"Why would they have an issue? You're the one rushing to judgement. Do you think they hate every sweet, intelligent, and highly successful woman who their son brings to dinner? Hell, you were competing against their son for a partnership. That puts you on the same playing field as their bouncing baby boy," Grace reasoned, suddenly breaking off to cover the mic on her phone.

Laurel couldn't make out any of the words.

"Is that Cynthia? Put her on the line. Maybe she'll be more helpful, because sweet isn't how I would describe a woman whose first thought at seeing a dead body was how it was going to affect her employment prospects." Laurel stood, wishing she'd taken her time in doing so. The blood rushed from her head, causing the room to spin round like a top. A glance in the mirror once the flashing lights dimmed told her that her makeup hadn't been disturbed in the slightest. "Do you think they'll ask where I went to college?"

"What the hell is wrong with an accredited online college? Get over yourself, Laurel." That was the thing with best friends. They didn't mince words. They also didn't let you get away with bullshit without calling you out on it. Laurel also realized that

Grace hadn't confirmed who she was with, which wasn't like
her. "You're making things more complicated than they have to
be, especially given that Sebastian Gallo was arrested for a brawl
at First Ave. I don't think the Gallos have room to talk about
their son's prospects."

Laurel had never thought to put things in perspective like
that, but it did make it a little easier for her to breathe. She
wondered how Grace had known about Sebastian, but she asked
her own question instead.

"Where are you, anyway?" Grace most likely wanted to
know how Laurel could be talking like this without Smith
overhearing her. "You sound like you're in a tunnel. Did you
lock yourself in the bathroom?"

"We came back to Smith's apartment. And yes, I'm in the
bathroom. He's in the bedroom getting dressed for the evening."
She tucked a loose strand behind her ear, having chosen to wear
her hair up tonight. It kept her heavy mane off her neck. "He,
uh, hadn't planned on spending the night. He didn't have a
change of clothes at my place. By the way, Detective Nielsen and
Detective Mancini stopped by my apartment last night. They
asked about Gareth and Cynthia. I don't know why, considering
Gareth wasn't even in town and Cynthia was at a business dinner
the whole time."

"My hunch is that Marilyn caved under the pressure and
spilled the beans regarding the argument Cynthia and Gareth
had early last week in the office."

Grace once again pulled the phone away to speak with
someone.

"Who are you with?" Laurel tried to listen even more closely
than before, but she couldn't make out who the other party was,
other than it was a man. "Grace, is there something you're not
telling me? I tell you everything."

"Yes." The answer was given so suddenly that Laurel thought she'd only imagined the reply in her head. "There is, but I can't tell you over the phone. Go and enjoy your dinner tonight with Smith's family. We'll talk tomorrow at the office when we get a minute."

And just like that, Grace disconnected the line without so much as a goodbye.

Laurel was still staring at her cell phone when Smith opened the door and walked into the bathroom, wearing a pair of black dress pants and a sweater that had to have been tailored just for him. The gray and black woven material formed itself to his upper body in such a way that it left little to the imagination, yet the pattern lay perfect. She almost pulled the pin and suggested they skip dinner to spend the rest of the night in his bed, but he beat her to the punch and spoke first.

"Everything okay in here?" Smith's worried gaze dropped to the phone in her hand.

"I don't know," Laurel answered honestly, wishing she could get Grace back on the line. Laurel had a strange feeling her friend wouldn't answer, and that caused another round of concern for her friend. "I think she was with a man."

"And that's unusual how?" Smith asked, his eyebrow cocked in amusement. "Grace is an attractive woman in her own right. Plus, someone mentioned to me the other day that she was having an intimate dinner with Rye Marshall."

"Rye Marshall? From Marshall Securities?" Laurel had truly thought her day couldn't get much worse, but she should know better than to tempt fate. "He's Manon Investments' top competitor. Grace would never do that to the firm. She has principles."

"Just like our compliance officer at Manon Investments wouldn't get involved with one of our top clients? Or that two of the analysts who were up for promotion wouldn't ruin their chances at partnership on an intimate relationship? Oh, and don't forget that one of those analysts is about to start up his own competing fund, splitting the two leaders on the board."

Laurel understood that the financial industry, as well as many others, was very cutthroat and bloodthirsty. Fortunately, it had never affected her personally.

Now?

She was screwed.

She'd gotten herself into a mess. Somehow, she knew all of the players very well in this little melodrama. She'd worked with the deceased. And she was the one to discover Brad Manon's dead body.

"Oh, no. This is bad. Really bad." Laurel pressed the home button on her phone, quickly reconnecting the call with Grace. "She's going to be Detective Nielsen's prime suspect if he finds out about this."

Smith stepped behind Laurel, attempting to massage the tension out of her shoulders. This position had both of them facing the mirror, but amazingly, she didn't notice any differences other than a man comforting a woman. They even looked good together.

"A candlelight dinner doesn't necessarily mean that Grace is involved with Rye," Smith said, attempting to smooth over her concern. "They could be close friends, for all we know. Or she could have been accepting a first-class meal in exchange for listening to his recruiting pitch. You know, that's not out of the question."

It still didn't look good in the grand scheme of things. Laurel closed her eyes as his magical fingers did their job, but it was short-lived. The endless ringing eventually went to Grace's voicemail.

"Grace, call me back the second you get this message. It can't wait until tomorrow."

Laurel didn't want to leave any message which might be construed as incriminating on a voicemail, just in case the police didn't know about Grace's so-called involvement with their competitor.

"She's an intelligent woman, Laurel." Smith pressed a kiss to her temple, something he'd never done before. He'd been showing her the different facets of his personality since Friday night, and there wasn't one she really disliked. She would have thought this was a problem, but Grace's counsel and Smith's assurance that everything would be alright had her believing them. "She'll be fine. And so will we, because I finally get to introduce the woman in my life to my family."

Laurel didn't take a step toward the door the way Smith had clearly thought she would, bringing him up short. There was something she needed to know first.

"You never intended for our relationship to be merely temporary, did you?"

Smith stared at her in the mirror a little too long for her comfort.

"No, I didn't."

For some reason, the confidence in his response had butter-flies setting up residence in her stomach. How had she missed all the usual signs?

"You…" Laurel cleared her throat, still coming to terms with the fact that he could have chosen any woman within his own social circle. Granted, she was also free to choose any man who respected and admired her for who she was, but he was proving to be all those things and more. She certainly couldn't hold the fact that he had money against him, could she? There was one glitch in this perfect scenario he'd concocted, not that she was looking for any more complex anomalies than the situation already had. She wasn't. "You're assuming I'm going to stay in Minneapolis after the company closes. What happens if I go to New York?"

Smith studied her, and she got the feeling that he was holding something else back that could affect their future. He was too unruffled by her question. It was as if he had some kind of inside information. Then again, she hadn't given him much confidence that she was open to something more. She was trying her hardest, though.

"Let's take this one day at a time." Smith leaned down so that he was eye level with her in the mirror. The faintest scent of his cologne enveloped her, for some reason causing her to believe that tonight might actually be a success. It helped that he gave her a boyish smile she'd never seen with a wiggle of his eyebrows. "Are you ready to meet my parents?"

"No," Laurel replied with as much confidence as he had regarding their relationship.

Her immediate response garnered the laugh she was hoping for, but her stomach still felt like a playing field for butterflies inside of a globe. He released her shoulders, stroking a hand down her arm and grabbing her hand. He went to guide her out of the bathroom she'd been in for the last fifteen minutes, but she quickly yanked him back when a thought occurred to her that might benefit the both of them.

"Would you do me a favor?"

"Anything."

The way Smith answered had Laurel's heartbeat stuttering against her chest. He hadn't even hesitated a split second, and his level stare had her wishing she'd brought up the option to spend the evening in bed. Having her meet his parents was important to him, though.

"Would you spill something down that expensive sweater of yours in the middle of dinner? You know, before I spill red wine on your mother's seventeenth century white French linen tablecloth?"

It was more than apparent Smith thought he'd heard her wrong, but when she didn't correct any of her verbiage, he began to smile.

It gave her hope that tonight would actually go well.

CHAPTER ELEVEN

DINNER HADN'T GONE quite as well as he'd hoped, but that had more to do with his father having the audacity to ask Laurel if she was going to work for Smith when he finally opened the doors to his own hedge fund. She'd stumbled at first, but recovered well. It was more than apparent the question had unsettled her.

It was the sole reason he hadn't brought it up to her himself when she'd asked him earlier what would happen to them as a couple should she move to New York. There was a time for such questions, and his father had no right just throwing it out on the table like a hunk of rotten flesh.

It most likely wouldn't have gone over well had he turned on his father or said that she wasn't going anywhere she didn't want to go. Either way, he would lose the initiative. He had no choice but to ignore the question as if it were asked by a petulant child.

Laurel would work with him, but not because they were involved. He wanted her simply because she would make the team a success. She was every bit as good in her sector as he'd been in his.

Honestly, she was one of the best retail analysts in the business. Hard work, dedication, talent, and a small amount of luck had gotten her to where she was today, and it would take her further should she decide to make the transition and work with him.

He needed someone with her experience, talent, and dedication.

But it was a battle when one didn't need to be fought. And it appeared—thanks to his father—that Smith would have to address it sooner rather than later. It was a conversation they would have in private, away from the judging eyes of his parents.

For now, they'd all retired to the living room where Nathanial Gallo was talking privately with Sebastian regarding the brawl he'd taken part in the other night. It had become a regular occurrence, but Smith was grateful that the attention was off his love life for a brief moment.

"Does Laurel drink coffee or tea?" his mother asked, gently resting a hand on his arm before he could join Laurel on the couch. She was having an in-depth conversation with his sister and brother-in-law. "I wasn't certain, so I made both."

"Ah, Mom, did I mention that you're my favorite parent?" Smith put an arm around his mother's shoulders, her attempt to make Laurel feel comfortable telling him that she approved. Alice Gallo didn't go to extra lengths for just anyone. She wrapped her arm around his waist in return. "And she's a coffee drinker."

"You've been seeing her for a while." Alice also wasn't one to beat around the bush. "You knew she didn't like peas at dinner. I know you don't want to hear this, but you're more like your father than you realize."

Only his mother would have noticed that he hadn't bothered to pass the vegetable to his left after he'd taken his own helping. Yes, he'd been with Laurel for three months, almost every evening with the exception of Sunday nights or when one of them needed to work late. They'd eaten quite a bit of takeout at his apartment, because she'd dug her heels in when he offered to cook for her one time. He would have to remedy that soon.

As for the reference to his father, well, his mother was right. Smith didn't want to hear that he was like his father in any other way other than dedication to his work. The man hadn't been much of a father, rarely having been involved in any of their childhoods beyond providing for them.

"Is Laurel the one?"

"Yes, she is."

Smith didn't hesitate to answer his mother's question, because he would never have brought Laurel here to meet his family had he any doubts at all. There were numerous reasons why he was careful about who he brought home, and none topped the other on his priority list. His father was usually critical of the smallest of imperfections, his brothers had a habit of bringing up embarrassing memories, and his mother usually tried to make more out of something casual.

But not this time.

Granted, his and Laurel's relationship began in a rather unique manner, but it didn't lessen what they'd created. The quality time they'd managed to accumulate over the last three months was equivalent to what most couples partake in a year. They connected on an extremely intimate level that would only grow stronger now that they'd made a commitment to strengthen their bond.

"I like her," Alice said with a smile, looking on as Laurel continued to talk to Samantha and Todd. As a matter of fact, her hands were starting to wave in the air as she described something, telling him she was becoming more and more comfortable as the evening wore on. "I'll be back with that coffee in a moment."

Smith felt rather than saw Solomon make his way from where the small bar was located, tucked discreetly on the far side of the room. His older brother had followed in their old man's footsteps, though not without the head for money to forestall the lingering effects of his habit. Solomon spent far more than he made through his law firm or what he received from his trust fund.

"I heard about Brad Manon's murder." Solomon stood next to Smith with a glass of whiskey in his hand. He pointed it toward Laurel. "She was the one who found his body, right?"

"Solomon, you don't want to steer this friendly conversation in that direction," Smith warned, slipping his hands in his pockets so that he didn't inadvertently do something that would upset their mother. "I'd like to keep this evening civil, if possible."

Laurel chose that moment to look his way, flashing him a satisfied smile. It turned out that neither one of them had spilled wine or anything else that would have caused her embarrassment. He had no doubt had she done so, she would have inadvertently hit his elbow while he was lifting a fork to his mouth.

"I was just pointing out that she's handling the situation well." Solomon took a drink of his whiskey. He had the bad habit of feigning to gather the right words for what he wanted to convey. "Those quiet types are the ones you have to watch out for, though."

And there it was.

The inevitable jab that had been brewing all evening just under the surface.

"Solomon, would you please be a dear and go back into the kitchen for some napkins?" Alice gave Smith a wink as she walked by with a tray full of a coffee carafe and several mugs. "Oh, and please take out the garbage that I left by the back door."

Solomon muttered a few curse words under his breath, but

he did so low enough so their mother couldn't hear him. He drained the rest of his whiskey and handed Smith the glass before doing their mom's bidding. She always had a way of getting her point across without having a violent confrontation. Had it escalated to an exchange of words, Solomon would be dragging his wounded ego around for a month.

Smith's cell phone rang, so he stepped out of the living room to take the call in private. He had multiple irons in the fire regarding his new business venture, but he'd also asked Meg to keep him apprised of the investigation should she hear anything through the grapevine. A quick look at the display told him the call had something to do with the latter, but the caller wasn't Meg.

"Josh?" Smith addressed their top trader, though Steve would take offense at that title. Either way, Josh always came through for Smith when trading a low volume stock. It was rare that he reached out for anything other than business. "Is everything okay?"

"No, man. I need a sizable favor." Josh always sounded as if he were on sedatives, but it was just his personality. He was laid back and didn't let anything or anyone get under his skin. Something had to be majorly wrong for him to call and ask for a favor like lightning out of the clear blue sky. "I'm going to need a criminal lawyer, and I was hoping you'd cover the retainer until I can pay you back."

Smith purposefully didn't reply right away, giving himself time to think through the various scenarios on how this could play out.

"Man, all my money is tied up in the new house and my wife's graduate degree. I can't afford this kind of shit right now." Josh was never one to care about privacy. The entire office was aware that he'd sunk a lot of cash into building a house out in

Edina. The town was listed as one of the wealthiest towns in America, and he'd been running in those circles for a couple years now. "My ass is going to land in jail if you don't help me out, Gallo. I promise I'm good on the backend. I'll take it out of my 401k if I have to."

"Josh, you know I could care less about the money. You can have whatever you need." Smith wasn't surprised when Laurel joined him in the formal dining room. "I want to know why you think you need a criminal lawyer, of all things."

Who? Laurel mouthed the word, wanting to follow at least half the conversation.

Josh.

"I met with Brad that night in the office, but I swear I didn't kill him. Smith, you've got to believe me. I thought I was in the clear when I'd heard about the surveillance videos being wiped clean, but they somehow got my vehicle coming and going from the garage a couple of hours before he died."

Smith rubbed the back of his neck to get rid of some of the tension, but it was a useless endeavor.

"Josh, why didn't you come clean with the police when you were questioned?"

"Because I didn't do it, man. I wasn't going to put myself at the top of the suspect pool just to clear my conscience. I didn't want the complications."

Josh wasn't one to lose his shit during times of stress, which was what made him one of the best traders in the industry. His panic was practically dripping out of the phone.

"Are the police at your house now?"

"No, but it's only a matter of time before they drag me in."

"Your best bet is to get out in front of this. I'll have my lawyer, Meg Preston, meet you at the station for the initial interview. I'll let her know the overview, but you're going to have to go into every detail with her. Tell her everything, Josh. And I mean everything. Don't leave a single thing out that could come back to haunt you later."

"I owe you."

Smith didn't bother to reply to that, because a desperate man was an unreliable man. The thing of it was, he believed Josh's claim of innocence.

"The police suspect Josh killed Brad?" Laurel was already shaking her head in denial. "He couldn't have…"

"I don't think he did, either." Smith located Meg's contact information and initiated the call. He continued to speak while the other end rang. "Josh swears he's innocent, but he was at the office the night Brad was killed."

"Why?" Laurel inquired with astonishment, prompting Smith to wish he'd asked that very question. "Josh and Brad were like cats and dogs being shoved into the same room together. They never mingled outside business hours."

It was well known that Paul had lured Josh over from the sell side. Brad hadn't wanted a wild card on the trading desk, but Paul had insisted they have someone with wider finance connections. Manon Investments got that and more through Josh, who was also very proficient at trading options.

A year into Josh's employment, Brad had a major turnaround in his position regarding the young trader. The two even begun socializing in the off hours with their wives. Of course, everything had gone south when Meredith discovered Brad was cheating on her with a hostess at their favorite restaurant.

"I don't know why the two met up that night, but I'm sure we'll hear all about it tomorrow." Smith turned his attention to Meg when she answered on the third ring. "Meg, I need a favor."

Smith spent another few minutes explaining who Joshua Green was in relation to Manon Investments. She went into detail as to why it wasn't in Smith's best interest that she represent anyone outside the two of them in regard to the same investigation, promising to send one of her partners who had just as much experience as she did with cases like these. Apparently, she'd only done so for Laurel as a favor to him.

"I think we should call it a night."

Smith slipped his cell phone back into his pocket, a sliver of unease taking root in his muscles. He was glad Laurel had decided to spend the night with him. He didn't want her going home alone.

"Your mother made me coffee," Laurel pointed out, though it was obvious he didn't have to twist her arm too hard to get her to agree with him. She did catch him off guard with her next statement, though. "Oh, I forgot to give you this."

Smith looked down and saw that she was holding one of those wipes for stains. He took it from her, but he wasn't sure why he would need it.

"It's for the edge of your sleeve." Laurel pointed toward the cuff of his dress shirt that showed from underneath his sweater. Sure enough, there was a stain of spaghetti sauce. "I started small, just in case I made it through dinner without spilling the wine."

Laurel flashed him a smile as she turned on her black flats, having refused to wear the heels he'd suggested. A flash of memory returned from when she'd laid her hand on his arm, having laughed at something he said that hadn't been humorous in the least. She'd actually dipped his sleeve into his food without anyone the wiser.

"You're a little minx, you know that?" Smith called out after her, confident that this family dinner had been an overall success.

Laurel tossed him a small wave over her shoulder as she continued into the living room. It was good to see her enjoy herself, but tomorrow was a new day. It wouldn't be easy going back into the same office where she'd found the body of Brad Manon. His previous unease hadn't dissipated, and he briefly considered asking her to take the day off. Everyone would understand if she did so, but he was already aware she wouldn't go for it, even if it served her own best interest.

It was obvious that tomorrow wasn't going to be the usual day at the office, but Smith had learned long ago to never assume the situation couldn't get worse. Josh was the perfect example.

Who would be next up to bat in this World Series of calamities?

CHAPTER TWELVE

L AUREL REACHED BACK and pulled her hair around so that the strands fell over her right shoulder. The elevator was taking its sweet old time arriving. It wasn't good to stand here idle, seeing as her thoughts were spinning around at a million miles per hour.

"No luck?"

She didn't have to ask Smith what he was talking about, considering he was already aware that she'd left Grace several messages this morning and had continued to try to reach her friend on the drive into the office. Smith had insisted they ride together. It had worked to her advantage, considering she'd been concentrating on trying to call Grace, but now it left her stuck here at the office without a vehicle should she need one.

"No. Cynthia hasn't heard from Grace, either." Laurel breathed a sigh of relief when the elevator doors gradually opened as if they had all the time in the world. Smith held his arm out against the door, allowing her to enter the carriage first. "If she's not here, I might need to borrow your car."

"Anything you need." Smith pressed the correct floor number before stepping back to join her. They had gotten ready together this morning, even saving water by using the shower at the same time. Actually, they hadn't saved any water in her estimate. It was cold by the time they were done. "Are you good to go?"

Smith was subtly asking if she was okay with the two of them walking into the office together. Sure, there had been numerous times in the past when they'd driven into the garage at the same time. It had been nothing but a coincidence then, but now that the word was out? It was on purpose and it made a statement.

"Yes, I'm fine." Laurel bit the side of her cheek as she pondered on what the next few minutes would entail. She hated being the center of attention in most situations. She was always able to work better flying under the radar, and that included her personal life as well. "Are you? I mean, are you sure you want to make our relationship public knowledge? We can still—"

She hadn't expected Smith to step forward and reach out to hit the stop button with the palm of his hand. But she was prepared for when he backed her up against the wall of the elevator, though her heart did race at the thought that they might be a little late for this morning's briefing if he didn't hurry.

"I took you to Sunday dinner to meet my family." Smith was so close that all she could do was stare into his dark eyes, so filled with arousal. "There is no going back for me, Laurel."

This weekend *had* changed everything.

She didn't want to admit that something good had come out of this tragedy. No one deserved to die the way Brad had, and it wasn't fair that he'd died at such a relatively young age. She would give anything to turn back the clock and not find him in such a brutally murdered fashion.

But there was no going back for Brad.

Just as there was no going back on this path she and Smith had found themselves on. Truthfully, it sounded as if he'd been parked there all along, waiting for her to give the all clear so that he could put the car in drive and press on the gas pedal.

Today? The sun was shining, her feet were up on the dashboard, and the wind was in her hair. No, she didn't want to go back even one miniscule mile.

Spending time with his family had made her realize they were no different than her own. As a matter of fact, Alice Gallo and Brenda Calanthe would most likely get along famously. It had been easy to see that Alice cherished her family, flaws and all. She'd doted on Smith, yet had been stern with Sebastian and his ridiculous antics.

As for Solomon, Alice had put him in his place when needed before showering him with praise on other matters. It was a tactic Laurel had employed with difficult clients on more than one occasion. Alice's son-in-law, Todd, had not been treated any differently than any of the other siblings.

It was clear to see that the only difference between the Gallos and the Calanthes was the addition of truckloads of currency…said to be the root of all evil. And that would only become a problem should Laurel allow it to happen.

"If you smear my lipstick again, you're going to have to cover for me at the meeting while I go to the restroom and freshen my makeup," Laurel whispered, wondering when the elevator had turned into a sauna. A shrill ringing sound suddenly came from somewhere outside the closed doors. No, she didn't want to change a thing right now other than getting them moving. "It's one thing to admit we're involved with one another, but it's another to be unprofessional in the elevator."

"And we wouldn't want that, now would we?" Smith asked, lowering his head until she felt the searing heat of his lips against the side of her neck. Excitement traveled through her at lightning speed, causing her to tighten her grip on her briefcase. She tilted her chin slightly to the right so that he had full access to her collarbone. The light nip from his teeth all but had her on edge. "I guess we'll have to continue this after the market closes."

One thing was a staple in the financial industry, and that was no one got any personal time during market hours. Stocks didn't stop trading because a person had a dentist appointment or got sick. That specific detail was hit home by the fact that the employees of Manon Investments were going into work on a Monday after the fund's portfolio manager had been murdered.

Laurel had time to even her breathing after Smith reactivated the elevator, the doors eventually gliding open to reveal Paul.

"Smith, I need to speak with you in my office. Right now."

Paul didn't wait for Smith to answer him, but instead, turned on the heel of his dress shoe and marched back through the opened glass doors. It was easy to see Marilyn in her usual spot, staring at her computer as if nothing unusual had occurred.

"Laurel?" Smith must have called her name a couple of times, because he was looking at her with concern. "Are you going to be alright?"

Laurel didn't want to set foot across the threshold, knowing the location of her office would take her directly down the same hallway leading toward the large office at the end of the corridor where she'd found Brad's dead body. Nausea rolled over her stomach as flashes of memory hit her like a sledge hammer repeatedly.

"Of course," Laurel finally managed to reply, holding her head high in spite of what lay before her. She tugged on her suit jacket to make sure it was firmly in place and took a deep breath. It was easier to divert her attention to the upcoming confrontation Smith was about to endure from Paul. It was more than obvious that he'd found out about Smith's future plans and the fact that they didn't involve Manon Investments. "The question is…are you going to be alright with Paul?"

Smith flashed her a confident smile, surprising her when he

leaned in for a kiss. Only he didn't press his lips to hers, not stopping until his warm breath was caressing her ear.

"After the innovative way we made my shower work out in our favor this morning, I'm ready for just about anything."

Laurel stared off unfocused after Smith as he strolled away, easily recalling how the hot water felt against her...

"I need to talk to you," Grace muttered rather harshly, not stopping as she walked past Laurel after getting off the elevator. She even shot a frustrated look over her shoulder as she rounded the corner to the left.

"Good morning, Marilyn."

Laurel greeted the older woman just as she did every other morning. Upon closer inspection, it was clear that Marilyn's eyes were bloodshot and her nose was pink from where she'd been wiping it with a tissue. A sudden wave of residual grief came over Laurel. She'd always compartmentalized things like this, but there were times it slipped out of one of those slots.

"It's just so different without him here," Marilyn whispered as her eyes welled up with more tears. She sniffled and wiped the tissue underneath her eyes. "And now Paul has so much on his plate now."

"This is when we have to be the strongest," Laurel advised gently, reaching over the wooden counter to pat Marilyn's hand in comfort. "Brad would want this company to continue in the wake of his passing."

Laurel figured Marilyn understood the way this industry worked, and that a hedge fund manager *was* the fund. Without him, it all disintegrated. Hopefully in the most organized fashion possible. Paul could try and bring another big name on board, but it was highly unlikely that would happen in time to keep the clients happy. The chances were that Paul would try to capitalize on the Gallo name in some fashion. Maybe even attempting to convince Smith to stay and take up the reins in Brad's place, at least in the short term. Laurel understood her words to Marilyn were rather empty, but the sentiment was there.

"Just so you know, I'm having lunch brought into the office today. I can't imagine what today will turn out being like." Marilyn cleared her throat and tossed her tissue into a trashcan she had underneath her desk. She sniffled one last time before straightening her shoulders, taking Laurel's advice about continuing their jobs regardless of their grief. "Meredith is stopping by around noon."

"Thanks for letting me know."

Laurel smiled sympathetically before walking toward her office. Her heels clicked on the marble tile before making contact with the plush carpet that lined the corridor. Unfortunately, her subconscious must have recalled that specific night. The hallway seemed to narrow with each step she took farther down the passageway, her focus solely on Brad's office door at the very end. It was closed with a small strip of yellow crime scene tape across the frame and an adhesive tamper seal at eye level on the knob side.

"Honestly, I'm surprised they even allowed us the ability to come in today."

Laurel rested a hand over her heart, which was now beating hard against her chest.

"Damn it, Cynthia," Laurel murmured, resisting the temptation to swing her briefcase at Cynthia, who'd silently appeared out of nowhere. "You scared the shit out of me, woman."

"God, you two take forever." Grace was standing in Laurel's open doorway, tapping her royal blue heel against the threshold. Her blonde hair wasn't as perfectly contained the way it usually was on any given workday. A few of her thick tresses had escaped the clip she used to keep her hair back, similar to the way Audrey Hepburn styled her hair back in the '60s. "I'm having a serious crisis here."

Cynthia handed Laurel a to-go cup from the café downstairs. She'd known they both would need the extra shot of espresso.

"Shut my door," Laurel ordered, closing the distance to her desk and setting her briefcase on her chair. The files she'd come in for Friday night sat directly in the middle of her desk, as if taunting more memories to return. She did her best to ignore them as she leaned against the corner of her desk. "Grace, I had to hear from Smith that you're involved with Rye Marshall. What the hell? I thought we were friends."

"Don't even go there with me, Miss It's Only Great Sex," Grace reprimanded, pacing the short distance to the window overlooking the busy street below. "Rye and I knew each other long before I came to work for Manon Investments. We, well, we were involved for a while back in college. And out of college, but it's been over for some time."

"Were you up front with Detective Nielsen about your former relationship with one of our top competitors?" Cynthia asked, having taken the guest chair. Hardly anything ever ruffled the woman, and she was in total control over her emotions this morning. Her call to Gareth must have gone well or the police were now working another angle besides Gareth Nicollet's harmless threat from last week. That angle could very well end up being Grace herself. "If so, you shouldn't have anything to worry about."

"That's just the thing." Grace spun around to do another loop. The carpet would likely lose its color from all her pacing, but it wasn't as if they were all going to be here in a year anyway. "I lied."

Laurel wasn't sure why she'd decided to take a drink of the vanilla latte Cynthia had brought at the precise moment. Grace's

admission had Laurel inhaling in disbelief, causing the unfortunate response of the hot liquid getting sucked down the wrong
tube. Her coughing fit didn't stop Cynthia from addressing the
major issue they now had to deal with in order to make sure
Grace didn't go to jail.

"Why the hell would you lie to the police?" Cynthia asked,
uncrossing her right leg from its comfortable position. She only
ever did that when something bothered her or got underneath
her skin. Fortunately, she snagged Laurel's coffee in the same
motion. "What were you thinking?"

Laurel managed to get herself somewhat under control before reaching for her vanilla latte again. A part of her wished
Cynthia had thought to add something stronger than an
additional espresso shot, but that wouldn't have been acceptable
in the office at seven o'clock on a Monday morning.

"I was thinking that I needed to protect Rye from suspicion," Grace practically spit back. She leaned up against the far
wall, having lost all the color in her face. That was evident by the
stark streak of blush on either cheek. "I was supposed to have
dinner with him Friday night, but he—"

"Back up a second," Laurel directed, now having received
enough oxygen in her lungs to join the conversation. "You said
you were involved with him a long time ago. So why were you
having dinner with him Friday, and what do you mean by
supposed to? Where was he?"

"One thing led to another a while back, but I didn't think it
was appropriate given our careers."

"I'm glad that thought actually crossed your mind," Cynthia
said wryly, sitting back in her chair with a shake of her head. No
one had ever promised her that her role as compliance officer
would be easy. "Do you know how this is going to look to that
detective? Laurel, you need to call that woman who sat with you

during your interview with Detective Nielsen. Grace is going to need someone with her when she explains why she wasn't exactly forthcoming during her session earlier."

Laurel realized that she couldn't do that for Grace, but that didn't mean Meg Preston still couldn't be able to have someone else handle this small problem. Okay, it wasn't so small, but it was still manageable.

"Wait," Laurel said, buying herself some time to figure out what she could say regarding Smith's lawyer. Meg had told Smith that it would be better for Josh to have another attorney. "Exactly why weren't you forthcoming, Grace? I mean, why did you lie for Rye in the first place? And why didn't you tell us what the hell was going on?"

"I know why she didn't say anything to *me* about the man." Cynthia must have had time to process the mess Grace had gotten herself into, though Laurel still needed time to catch up. Cynthia crossed her legs and settled back into her chair. "I would have told her that she was crazy, even by my rather unorthodox standards. It's one thing to mix business and pleasure, but quite another thing totally when you could be accused of corporate espionage and murder."

"That's not fair."

"You didn't say anything to me when you found out I was seeing Smith," Laurel pointed out, ignoring Grace's outburst. She was rightfully upset, but she still hadn't explained why she would lie for the man. It made Laurel realize how fortunate she was that Smith had told the truth regarding her alibi. "Oh, and I met his parents at Sunday dinner…just for the record."

"I didn't say anything about you and Smith, because it was all in-house and rather entertaining. You…wait. You met his parents? Oh, my God!" Cynthia had what Laurel referred to as the Cheshire grin, though her lips were as red as her nails. The color went really well with her jet-black hair that was framed toward her face. "Have you finally seen the blinding light and—"

"Could we focus here, please?" Grace practically yelled, her hands now in fists at her side. "Rye was supposed to come to my apartment for dinner Friday night. He was running late. He got to my place around eleven o'clock."

Laurel and Cynthia both stared at Grace as the time she mentioned sunk in deep. As deep as the hole she was about to find herself in with the police.

"Grace, you realize that the time frame is—"

"I know what the time frame was for Brad's murder, which is why I lied to the police. And I'm not sure I'm going to say anything further." Grace tucked the blonde curl back behind her ear and closed her eyes to regain her composure. "Rye swears he had a flat tire driving from his house to my apartment. I believe him, but the police wouldn't. Why would they? He'd be a perfect suspect. They could wrap this whole thing up with a tidy little bow."

Laurel tilted her cup and drank a healthy amount of her vanilla latte. Three intelligent women had somehow allowed three men to screw up their lives. *That wasn't fair.* She swallowed back her guilt at thinking something so negative about Smith. He'd done everything in his power to make sure she was alright this weekend. He'd somehow barreled past the barriers she'd had in place, and their future looked bright and shiny compared to some.

Well, somewhat bright.

They still needed to address the fact that Smith would like for her to work with him after Manon Investments eventually closed their doors. She wasn't sure that was all too good of an idea, but she also couldn't see herself leaving Minneapolis for New York if there was another offer on the table. For one, there was her mother. Two, she and Smith had started to build something that could actually be called a solid foundation of sorts.

"He wasn't dripping with blood, was he? I mean, you should still tell the police," Cynthia said, sipping her coffee in between her bit of advice and her insane question. "The city has a million security cameras. Surely there's a way to prove that Rye had a flat tire somehow."

"And what if Brad's real killer figures out that I can't give Rye an alibi? What if he or she somehow manages to wipe the footage off those cameras, as well? What then?"

"I think we're giving this murderer too much credit." Laurel had never been a huge conspiracy theorist. Normally, neither was Grace, but stress could do strange things to a person. The thing of it was, they were all under a great amount of stress losing one of their own. It didn't help that the police were treating them all as suspects, but they also had a job to do. "You should—"

A knock came at the door, startling all three of them into silence.

"Yes?" Laurel called out after a moment, sharing a look between the two other women. The stock market didn't open until nine-thirty eastern time, and they were still around five minutes out from their daily morning meeting. She quickly walked back around her desk and dug out Meg's business card. "Grace, here is Meg's number. Give her a call and see if she can recommend someone to accompany you down to the station."

"Laurel?" Marilyn poked her head around the door. Her red nose indicated she'd yet to really gather her composure. "Paul is asking for everyone to assemble in the trading room as soon as possible."

All three women waited until Marilyn closed the door before

speaking.

"No," Grace responded to Laurel's offer, doing her best to tame her loose strands before dealing with whatever Paul was about to throw their way. Laurel couldn't help but wonder if it had anything to do with Smith. "Keep the business card. I'm not saying anything to anyone. My imagination was running away with me. No one is going to try and frame Rye or implicate me in any way."

Laurel and Cynthia attempted to talk over one another, both of them agreeing that Grace needed to reconsider her stance on providing Rye with an alibi. Cynthia even added on that Paul would eventually discover that Grace was involved with his biggest competitor and call her onto the carpet, per se. It was better to face this head on like Laurel should have done with Smith from the very beginning.

"I appreciate what you're trying to do, but I honestly think silence is the best course of action here." Grace took a deep breath before stepping toward the door. "Let's hope we're being called together right now because there was a break in the case, and they caught the suspect. Maybe the police have captured Brad's killer, and then we can all get back to our lives without any more drama."

One by one, they filed out the door. Laurel couldn't help but glance over her shoulder at the yellow crime scene tape strewn across the entrance to Brad's office along with that official-looking seal with two signatures scrawled on it with a sharpie. It still wasn't real that he was gone, and it was certainly harder to accept that his demise had been in such a horrific fashion.

Grace was right in a way. Everything could return to some-what normal operations with an arrest and a decent plan for the future. Laurel wasn't sure what that blueprint looked like at this very moment, but it would be a start to put the Power Point up and get a glimpse of the design.

Would it hold New York City?

Or would Smith and the life he offered be the centerpiece of her future?

CHAPTER THIRTEEN

S MITH NOTED THE numerous employees who entered the trading room for this impromptu meeting. Their daily briefing usually included only the traders and analysts. Paul asked for everyone to join them, meaning either an announcement was on the way or the police had contacted him with an update on Brad's murder.

It was most likely the former, because Smith had been in Paul's office for the last ten minutes. No phone call had interrupted their discussion nor had Marilyn conveyed any message that would indicate otherwise.

The beautiful woman he was seeking finally walked into the trading room, and a spike of satisfaction shot through him when her gaze immediately sought his. The waves of her chestnut hair hung over her right shoulder, telling him that she was still somewhat tense regarding these unusual circumstances. He was pleased when she weaved her way toward him through the additional employees standing around the large trading desk.

"How did your meeting go with Paul?" Laurel asked with concern, crossing one arm around her waist as she held a disposable coffee cup from the downstairs café. "Did he find out about your future plans?"

"Yes, but those might be changing in light of new information."

Paul had every right to be angry regarding Smith's decision

to start up his own firm. With that said, the manner in which Paul learned of those future plans hadn't been conducted the way Smith had intended. He had given assurances that he had no intention of stealing clients, but that promise would eventually fade given the fact that Manon Investments would no doubt close their doors at some point in the not too distant future.

"What does that mean?" Laurel asked, her eyes skimming over everyone in attendance. She most likely noticed that Josh was missing. She bit her lower lip, taking with it some of her pink lipstick. "Changes for you or Manon Investments? Is that what Paul wants to discuss?"

"I don't know what Paul is going to say today, but he does want to sit down with me later to go over some possibilities that could save a lot of the staff their jobs." Smith had employed one of the best head hunters in the business, but her services might not be needed if Paul offered Smith the ability to choose from the employees of Manon Investments. It would be in everyone's best interest, but Smith understood how that would ultimately look to Detective Mancini as the investigating officer. It would only cause the man to narrow his focus, as if it wasn't limited enough by all the intrigue going on around here. "Were you able to talk to Grace?"

"Yes, but we'll discuss that at home." Laurel shifted closer to Smith when Vern and Blair chose to stand right next to them. Laurel lifted the coffee cup to her lips while shooting Smith a warning glance. He was still focused on her use of the word *home*, sporting a bit of a smile. She lowered her voice to barely a whisper. "Have you heard from Josh?"

Paul began speaking before Smith could answer her, though he wouldn't have been able satisfy her curiosity.

Josh had been radio silent.

"First, I want to thank everyone for coming in today," Paul

said, speaking loud enough so that everyone could hear him over the whir of the numerous computers lining the trading desk. He paused long enough for everyone to give him their undivided attention. "Brad would want Manon Investments to proceed and put the needs of its clients first…even above his own death."

Silence blanketed the trading room, though Smith couldn't help but notice that Steve wasn't buying the emotional speech that was being given. As a matter of fact, the man seemed rather angry.

"I called you all to this meeting to clear the air and to ask that you do the same." Murmurs of curiosity rose. Paul raised his hand to hush everyone as he continued to speak. "It was our dream that Manon Investments be much like a family. We strived every day to make this your second home. Let's face it. We all work crazy hours, spending more time with each other than many of our own families."

That got a few chuckles from the administrative staff, but it was evident that some of the analysts and other employees didn't have the same line of thinking when it came to their environment. It wasn't a surprise to Smith when someone commented on that fact.

"Paul, get on with it." Steve had been leaning forward in his chair, resting his elbows on his knees. He usually dressed in black pants and a white buttoned-down shirt, though minus the tie. Today, he wore a pair of jeans and a long-sleeved blue shirt that had seen better days. "Say what you want to say, but don't try and change the fact that this place has turned into any other firm out there. We're all cutthroat, looking out for our own asses. It's why Josh is still down at the station being interrogated by the police."

Smith rested a hand on Laurel's lower back when she audibly inhaled her surprise. Honestly, he was quite taken aback that

Josh was still at the station.

"Steve, all I'm saying is that we need to rely on one another. No one should ever feel that they need to keep secrets in light of—"

"And why wouldn't they feel the need to protect themselves?" Steve rubbed his eyes in frustration before leaning back in his chair and spinning around so that he could call out those in question. "Josh was right here in the office the night Brad was murdered."

"Steve," Paul warned, most likely having wanted to be the one to share that bit of information.

"Vern was made an offer to work for Marshall Securities." Steve didn't heed Paul's advice. "And Cynthia, well, let's not forget she's involved with one of our clients who was overheard threatening Brad's life."

"Casting stones is never a good idea when you live in a glass house," Cynthia warned, her calm demeanor still set in place. She didn't even blink at the fact that Steve called her out in front of the entire firm. "One, my personal life is none of your business. Two, it's my understanding your own brother-in-law is the one who Paul was considering bringing on as another managing partner."

Cynthia's announcement drew another round of murmurs and all eyes were now back on Paul, looking for a reaction.

"Yes," Paul announced, nodding his head in Cynthia's direction at her defense to Steve's accusations. "Cynthia is right, and I gave her permission to share that information in case I wasn't here this morning in light of Josh's situation. I'm heading down to the station after this meeting to see if I can help alleviate the situation in any way. To enlighten you on my decision to bring on another managing partner, Brad wanted to concentrate solely on the portfolio of stocks. He was in total agreement to bring someone else on board with the clout to garner more assets under management. Steve's brother-in-law works out of London, and he was the perfect choice to head up the international side of the business. Of course, things have now changed quite a bit. Please understand that the confidentiality of such a decision was not to keep you in the dark, but for the board to decide if it was in the company's best interest to go forward with such a resolution at this given time."

"You say that now, but that's because we all know Manon Investments will close its doors in less than eighteen months."

"Steve, is there something else you want to get off your chest?" Paul asked bluntly, apparently not willing to play the man's game any longer. "I called this meeting to let those who—"

"You mean you want the rest of us to spill our secrets, but keep your own." Steve apparently had some deep-seated anger over something that not everyone was aware of, including Smith. It was something he would have to address with Paul should they end up working together in the future. There was no doubt that man could weave his way in and out of high net worth individuals as if he were a string of diamonds. "No thanks, Paul. I'll take my own chances with the police."

There was clearly something more going on between these two men that had somehow managed to stay hidden amongst the carnage.

Everyone had fallen silent at the exchange.

"Brad's death has been a shock to all of us. Our reactions to this and how we choose to go forward will define Manon Investments in the forthcoming days."

Paul did his best to salvage what was left of his speech. He'd lost control of the situation, but he successfully managed to spin it around by lifting everyone's spirits and clarifying how relying on each other was paramount. Trust and honesty were thrown into the mix, but the end result was that Paul would do whatever was in his power to make sure everyone came out on top at the end of the road.

"That was a beautiful speech, Paul. Thank you."

Smith wasn't surprised at Meredith Manon's presence. He'd seen her quietly step inside the trading room, careful not to call attention to herself as Paul wrapped up the meeting. Smith was quite shocked that she would come to the office when she'd steered cleared of this place for the last two years.

Her words were like a beacon in the dark.

The staff immediately gathered around her, giving their condolences. It didn't matter that she hadn't been married to Brad in many years.

"Well, this is uncomfortable," Blair mumbled as she walked past them on her way to join everyone else.

Blair pasted on a fake smile as she stood next to Grace, who just happened to be happily edged out of the crowd. There were a few stragglers who seemed to hesitate on what to do in this situation, but most eventually followed. The trading desk phones had already been ringing with news on the futures and other markets, so it wasn't a surprise that Steve stayed behind to answer them. He didn't seem to mind, though. It was business as usual for him.

"Why is she here?" Vern asked to no one in particular, but he seemed to expect Smith or Laurel to answer seeing as they were the only ones left on his side of the room. "Come on. They've been divorced for years."

"Meredith and Brad were still close, though," Laurel pointed out softly, her compassionate gaze landing on the grieving woman. "Losing someone you were that close with can't be easy. You should cut her a break, Vern. There is some blood left in those veins, right?"

Smith rubbed his tongue over his teeth, denying himself the privilege of coming to Laurel's defense when Vern scoffed at her light scolding. He didn't join the others, but instead, walked over to the trading desk and pulled out a chair to sit next to Steve.

"Well, he's off my fucking list, along with Steve."

"What list?" Laurel asked distractedly, still holding the disposable coffee cup close to her chest. Her concerned gaze was focused squarely on Meredith, but her follow up observation wasn't on the grieving woman as he'd thought. "Smith, this can't be good."

Josh was standing behind the gathered crowd, looking anything but relieved that he wasn't at the station. As a matter of fact, the anger that flushed his cheeks might very well land his ass back there.

"Are you seriously showing your face here after what you've been doing these past few months?"

"Josh," Steve called out a warning, standing up so fast that his chair rolled back a good six feet. The phone was still in his hand, hanging down at his side. "Don't do this."

"You're fucking the ex-wife of your boss…the one who was found dead three days ago," Josh said accusingly, glaring at Steve as if he were responsible for the man's murder. Maybe he was. Either way, the entire office was now filled in on another possible scenario. "Did you do it, Steve? Did you kill Brad Manon or was it her, you fucking coward?"

CHAPTER FOURTEEN

"**D**ID YOU HEAR that Josh quit?"

Laurel looked up from the quarterly report she'd been reading over to find Grace standing in her office doorway with a cup of sanity. Her blonde hair was perfectly pulled back in a French twist, not giving away her previous panic over Rye Marshall's whereabouts last week, for which she had supplied an alibi.

It was hard to believe ten whole days had passed since Laurel had found Brad's body in his office. How could there be no leads, especially given that so many people had motive to see him dead? There wasn't such a thing as the perfect murder. Or had unicorns come back in vogue when she hadn't been looking?

"I figured Josh would make that decision, considering his baggage," Laurel shared, wishing things could have been different. After Josh had found out that Steve had been having an affair with Meredith, it had certainly ended their previous friendship, but it had also damaged their working relationship beyond repair. "At least the police have cleared Gareth regarding that threat Marilyn had taken out of context."

So many things had happened over the course of the week, but a lot of it beneficial to those she cared about. Cynthia had decided to end things with Gareth, considering their roles in the construct of the business. It wouldn't surprise Laurel to find out that Gareth was pulling his money from the fund, just so that there wasn't any conflict. He didn't seem to realize that wasn't the only reason Cynthia had backed off of their affair. She appeared content with her decision, though, and that was all that mattered to Laurel.

Paul was around the office more, giving speeches to anyone he thought would benefit from his wisdom. He'd become somewhat philosophical of late. It wasn't a bad thing, but it was a bit much to take when he tried to recreate the old atmosphere from years prior that had died a brutal death along with Brad. Unfortunately, there was no going back to those initial days of the firm in its infancy.

"I'm worried about Cynthia." Grace handed Laurel one of the coffees she'd been carrying, not bothering to take a seat. The market was open, trades were being negotiated, and nothing got in the way of the daily grind. "I think she's having a harder time with her decision than she lets on. Are you free Thursday night? I was hoping we could take her out for drinks."

"Absolutely." Laurel missed their time together, but nothing had been the same since Brad's death. "And thanks for the java."

Grace lifted a hand in acknowledgement as she walked out of the office, leaving behind a faint scent of her favorite perfume. She hadn't said a word about Rye since last Monday. It was obvious that the police hadn't realized that Grace and Rye weren't together that night or else they both would have been called in for more questioning. At least, that was the current working theory she was going off of.

Speaking of calls, Laurel's cell phone rang. She'd left it in her purse, which happened to be underneath her desk. It made a hollow buzzing sound, followed by the familiar ring. Who would be calling her personal number at ten o'clock on a Monday morning? Even her mother knew to call the office when Laurel was at work.

"Hello?" Laurel had come very close to not answering the number displaying on the phone, not recognizing the digits. The only reason she swiped the bar to the right was because of the pending investigation. Detective Nielsen had reached out to her twice regarding that horrible night, looking for further details. All of his questions had been put through Meg and approved. "This is Laurel."

"Laurel, this is Alice. I know you're at the office, but Smith wouldn't transfer me to your line." Smith's mother sounded as cheerful as she had last night, though that might have had more to do with the second glass of wine she'd had after dinner. "I was wondering if you'd like to go shopping with me on Saturday for the charity ball we'll both be attending."

Laurel hadn't been too pleased when Smith had answered for her, saying that they would be honored to attend the formal function to pull in money for one of the local hospitals. It wasn't that she didn't want to support the cause, but those personal insecurities of hers had reared their ugly heads. She hated feeling out of her element.

"That sounds like fun," Laurel replied, not having a choice but to accept unless she wanted to offend Alice. Honestly, it didn't sound like any fun at all. Laurel would most likely spend the entire day watching everything she said and did, all the while wondering if she was going to have a heart attack from the anxiety. She was already going to hell, but she'd rather delay the trip as much as possible. "Let me know where and when, and I'll be there."

"Fantastic," Alice exclaimed, clearly ecstatic over Laurel's acceptance. It caused her to flood with guilt, and now her temples throbbed with an oncoming headache. "I'll text you the time and place. We can meet there and do brunch, too. I'm looking forward to spending the day with you, Laurel."

She rested her forehead on the desk in defeat after Alice disconnected the call.

"I take it that was my mother?"

Laurel gave Smith a thumb up, not moving an inch because the coolness of the wood surface was doing wonders for her headache. This past week had been…well, almost perfect. Too perfect, to be honest. It truly scared the shit out of her, because she never would have thought they could have made their relationship work due to their professional entanglement. It somehow made the days and nights simpler, while allowing them to smoothly integrate themselves into each other's daily lives.

There was only one thing she hadn't done. And that was to introduce Smith to her mother.

"You know, she doesn't have fangs," Smith murmured, having quietly made his way from the doorway to her desk. He must have walked around the back of her chair, because his strong fingers began to knead the tension out of her shoulders. She might be able to handle a day with his mother if it meant this type of royal treatment. "And she thinks you have great taste in shoes, whatever that means."

"You're just trying to placate me into going," Laurel mumbled around a groan when his thumb pressed against a knot in the muscle of her shoulder blade. "I already said yes, but you can keep doing whatever it is you're doing as an installment payment."

Smith's rich laughter filled the air, and she realized that she'd heard him laugh more in the last week than the last three and a half months.

Her mom was going to love him a bit too much, and that was the sole reason Laurel had been putting off the introductions. Brenda Calanthe's endorsement meant Laurel could commit one hundred percent to the man standing behind her.

And that scared the hell out of her.

"I didn't just stop by your office to talk about my mother taking you shopping." Smith leaned down and pressed his warm lips against the back of her neck before stepping away. He surprised her when he made his way around to the front of her desk and took a seat in one of the guest chairs. "We need to talk."

And here it was…the gauntlet. This was the exact reason Laurel had been avoiding introducing him to her mother.

The talk.

Grace should have put a shot of something strong in Laurel's coffee.

"Josh resigned early this morning. I want to hire him."

Well, it was rare that Laurel was caught behind the cart, but that appeared to be the case. Her stomach was still kind of nauseated, but she managed to respond without sounding like an idiot.

"Hire him? You're still around nine months out from opening your doors, aren't you? The man has to make a living somehow, and I doubt that he's going to want to be unemployed for that long a period considering the house he just had built and the debt that goes along with that whole mess."

Laurel wasn't even sure why Smith was soliciting her advice. They had yet to discuss the fact that he wanted her to work for him.

"What if I could make it so that he had a temporary position, prepping the ground so to speak, before coming to work for me full time? You've worked with Josh for years. He's damned good at his job. Honestly, the best I've ever seen."

"Smith, you're not here to talk about Josh, are you?"

"I want you at my firm."

Laurel's heartrate stuttered at his forthcoming response, but she managed to save herself from entering a discussion she wasn't ready to have when Marilyn appeared in the doorway with a questioning look.

"Smith, someone is here to see you by the name of Catherine Greenlee. Her appointment was with Paul, but she stated she wants to see you first."

It was obvious that Marilyn didn't like Catherine Greenlee, and Laurel could relate. She was one of their high net worth individuals who ran in the same circles as the Gallo family. Unfortunately, the woman didn't contain one ounce of human decency like Smith's family encompassed. It was people like the Greenlees that made Laurel reluctant toward entering that type of lifestyle around those kinds of scavengers.

"I'll be there in a moment. Please ask her to wait for me in my office." Smith waited for Marilyn to walk away, giving him the privacy he clearly wanted for what he had to say regarding their previous conversation. His dark eyes met hers with that familiar intensity she was coming to expect from him. It still caused her heart to flutter in anticipation. "I want to make myself crystal clear."

Laurel wasn't expecting Smith to walk around the desk, holding out his hand for her to take as he guided her to her feet. Something told her that he was about to take a giant step forward, and she wasn't so sure her Garavani heels could follow suit. Catherine Greenlee was the perfect example of why doing so wouldn't be a good idea.

"Don't think for a second this gets you out of our conversation," Smith warned, his patience apparently running thin at her hesitancy. She couldn't really blame him, considering they'd spent almost every night at his apartment since they'd been forced to make their relationship public. They'd stayed at her place last night, but that was because she'd worn the couple of business suits she'd hung up in his closet. That in and of itself had been a pretty big step for her. "I'm serious, Laurel. I didn't want to do this here, but the look on your face makes it evident I couldn't wait."

"You can wait. There's no need for the Olympic pace."

Laurel swallowed around the lump in her throat, terrified he was about to say something he couldn't take back. She could admit that quietly sleeping with him without the world knowing had given her the best of both worlds. He had no idea what it was like to live with expensive student loans, helping her mother out financially, and working harder than any other employee for a partnership because she didn't have the right surname to be automatically included. The Catherine Greenlees of the world didn't open their arms and take anyone into their circle. Not for any reason. She would always be outside to those select few.

"I don't want to wait, sweetheart."

Alice Gallo had opened her arms, though.

"You should wait," Laurel encouraged as she struggled to maintain her composure. She wasn't one to get nervous in situations like this, but he was about to talk about their future. "Give it some more thought. We're working, and we promised Paul that we would—"

"We're having a discussion, Laurel. We're not fucking on the desk."

Laurel had to bite her tongue at the thought that she'd rather be doing the latter, because it was in those precious hours when she felt whole. Reality was what made her second-guess herself.

"Catherine Greenlee is waiting for you." Laurel would have taken a step back, but her chair was in the way. "It's not good for business to keep someone of her ilk waiting, especially one who has the kind of money she has to invest in your future hedge fund."

"You are something else." Smith's lips curled in a small smile as he cupped the side of her face with his warm hand. She was going to short-circuit if he didn't stop. "I had planned on an intimate dinner with rose petals and champagne. There was going to be—"

"We can still do that," Laurel urged, tamping down the need to escape. "There's nothing to say we can't postpone this talk until—"

"Laurel, I want you to stay in Minnesota after the doors close on Manon Investments."

Well, that was straightforward. And not nearly as terrifying as she thought this topic would be in the grand scheme of things. "I want you here with me, and I want you as my retail analyst."

"And you believe we can work seamlessly together while still seeing one another?" Laurel asked, able to breathe a little better now. "I'm not saying it can't possibly work, but there are—"

"It can work with you as my wife."

And there went all the oxygen in the entire room.

What had he expected? She'd been upfront with him all along that she wasn't sure the two of them were right for one another. It didn't matter that Alice Gallo wanted to take her shopping, or that Nathaniel Gallo had been elated when she'd challenged him at a game of chess last night. None of those things prevented flashing lights from dancing in front of her vision as she grappled with Smith's marriage proposal.

Only it wasn't a *down on one knee* proposal, per se.

Was it?

Laurel reached up and grabbed his wrist, needing something solid to hold onto. He'd somehow become her anchor over the past four months without her ever realizing how entangled they'd become in each other's lives.

"That didn't come out right," Smith murmured, resting his other palm on her other cheek. "When I properly ask you to marry me, Laurel, it certainly won't be in the office. What I need you to know is that I do love you. All of you. From your odd sense of humor to the fact that you allow your neighbor to keep her breastmilk in your freezer. I love that you never allow my father to intimidate you and that you secretly adore that my mother is taking you shopping. And let's not forget your heel fetish, because sometimes it's the only thing getting me through those daily meetings. I love you, Laurel Calanthe, and I want you to stay in Minneapolis because you love me, too."

CHAPTER FIFTEEN

I T WAS CLEAR that Smith had stunned Laurel with his declaration of love. Honestly, he'd shocked himself with his unorthodox timing. The office was no place to have this conversation.

"Don't say anything quite yet," Smith directed when she parted her lips in surprise. He wasn't finishing this discussion here. "Let's manage to get through today, and we'll talk more tonight over those rose petals."

"You can't just drop a bomb like that and—"

"Smith? I only have thirty minutes this morning," Catherine stated from her sudden presence in the doorway. It was a wonder that she wasn't tapping the toe of her high heel. There was absolutely no remorse for interrupting his and Laurel's private conversation. In fact, her striking blue eyes had a gleam of satisfaction shining brightly as her gaze skimmed over Laurel in judgement. "I saw the receptionist come this way to deliver my message, so I figured you were back this way somewhere."

"Catherine, you can wait for me in the foyer or my office." Smith dropped his hands from Laurel's beautiful face, but he remained close. Catherine's stare followed his movement, landing on where his fingers rested on Laurel's hip. "I'll be there in a moment."

Catherine seemed to weigh his words, almost as if she were going to argue with the merit of his edict. Though Manon

Investments dealt with high net worth individuals all the time, it was rare that the clients were downright rude. It was more than apparent that she had an agenda here, but he wasn't about to play her childish games. She was worse to deal with than a pit of ravenous vipers.

"Fine," Catherine responded, though it was clear she wasn't okay with his decision to place her in a box. He wouldn't deny that she was stunning in a red pantsuit, with beautiful accessories that screamed garish wealth. It was too bad she couldn't buy a bit of class with the money in her bank account. She didn't hold a candle to Laurel. "I'll see if the receptionist can manage a decent cup of coffee."

Smith sighed and rubbed his eyes in frustration.

"Well, this day isn't going as planned." Smith turned so that he could lean back against Laurel's desk while facing her. He wanted to gauge her reaction and ensure that she wasn't about to book a flight to New York. "What are your thoughts, little minx?"

"That you should really go and take that meeting before she burns down the building." Laurel pulled her hair over her right shoulder. Her gesture spoke volumes. She grabbed the coffee that had been on her desk as if it were a lifeline. "I have a feeling that she's going to pull her funds early and reinvest somewhere more responsive to her needs."

"And you'll still be here when I'm through?"

"Of course, I will."

Laurel seemed to take offense at his question, but he was on a playing field that wasn't quite level. His family had welcomed her into their home. The intimacy they shared had become even more familiar, if that were even possible. Their relationship had gradually moved forward in the most gratifying way.

"If you're wary of us working together, then I'll just have to move the firm to New York."

Smith had learned early on in his life that nothing couldn't be overcome with enough effort. He would move mountains if it meant keeping her in his life.

"Smith, you can't be serious about that—"

"No?" Smith asked, quite taken aback that she would question such an announcement. "If your hesitation lies in us working together while being personally involved, then I'll move my firm to New York. You said yourself that you have prospects lined up in the city, so that's where we'll go. I'll have my lawyers start the process by the end of the business day."

"Smith, stop," Laurel exclaimed as she held up one hand, setting down the coffee she'd just picked up. She was also shaking her head and frowning at him as if his proposal was ludicrous. "Can't you see that this is part of the problem? Money can't solve everything."

"No, it doesn't. Wealth has nothing to do with this, and until you realize that, we'll continue to circle this issue in an endless loop." Smith didn't bother to point out that money *did* make things a hell of a lot easier. That wouldn't help his cause at the moment. He needed to stick to the facts, because that was the only way he had a chance to get her to see that what they had was more important than anything monetary. "It's our decisions that affects our present and future. Us. Money is just a byproduct of our labors. We're not what we do."

Smith wanted to delve deeper into this conversation, but Paul would inevitably come looking for him. This was too important of a discussion to skim over. What else could he do or say that would cause Laurel to see that the only thing standing in their way was her own insecurities?

"Our jobs, where we live, what we make…take it all away. We're still two people who've connected in the most intimate way possible." Smith slowly reached out to touch her beautiful face, having not one doubt that she belonged in his life. "You are so confident in every other aspect of your life except for when it comes to me."

There was nothing left to say in this moment, because anything else he tried to convey would just be lost in the day to day operations that awaited them.

"We'll talk more tonight," Smith said softly, gently pressing his lips against her forehead. "You know me well enough that I'm not a man to give in at the first sign of troubled waters."

TAKE IT ALL *away. We're still two people who've connected in the most intimate way.*

Smith's words continued to echo in Laurel's mind over and over again until she couldn't take another moment alone in her office. She grabbed what was now a cold cup of coffee that Grace had supplied her with and went in search of some type of moral support.

Could it really be that simple?

She considered herself a highly intelligent person. Hell, she could even checkmate Nathaniel Gallo in five moves on the chess board when he'd underestimated her as a player. So how was it that she couldn't get out of her own way to claim the happiness that Smith was obviously offering her with his whole heart?

Marilyn was at her desk, typing vigorously away on her keyboard. A quick peek in the trading room showed Steve on the phone, with Vern sitting in the other seat and helping out the best he could, given that Josh had resigned from the firm and left them in a lurch. Blair was in her office on the other side, but

Grace was nowhere to be found.

Laurel detoured into the kitchen, taking the white lid off the plastic cup before warming it up in the microwave. She then covered the rim before seeking out Cynthia, who was almost always in her office.

Sure enough, Cynthia was focused on whatever document was displayed on her monitor. The black rimmed reading glasses matched the color of her hair and both were striking against her red lipstick. How could she look so put together when Laurel was practically coming apart at the seams?

"Am I materialistic?" Laurel asked, taking the guest chair across from Cynthia. "Seriously, do I put a value on money where there shouldn't be any?"

"You're only materialistic when it comes to high heels, as well you should be. Especially considering your predilection for high-end brands." Cynthia continued to scroll through the document she was viewing on the bright display, not even bothering to look Laurel's way. "Do I think you give too much deference to the wealthy? Absolutely."

Laurel both admired and loathed Cynthia's bluntness.

"Smith's currently in a meeting with Paul and Catherine Greenlee. He, um…well, he said he loved me before he left my office and referenced me as his future wife."

Now that bit of news garnered Cynthia's attention, who slowly allowed her chair to turn toward her desk. She ever so carefully removed her glasses and held them gently in her hands as she let Laurel's words soak in.

"Please tell me that you reciprocated his declaration and concurred with his views toward the future Mrs. Gallo."

Cynthia closed her eyes in disbelief when Laurel didn't respond. What could she say? That she was scared shitless her entire life was about to change, and she could lose the person she was before she met Smith? She wasn't even sure she remembered who Laurel Calanthe was before meeting Smith Gallo. Focusing on her career had been much easier than the crossroads she currently found herself at today.

"In my defense, Catherine Greenlee sought Smith out in my office before I could formulate an appropriate response," Laurel said, stretching the truth just a bit. She leaned forward in the chair to justify her reasoning. "I'm not about to confess my undying love in an office building with Catherine Greenlee in attendance to disapprovingly witness a private moment that should be cherished."

"So you do love the infamous Smith Gallo?" Cynthia tilted her head just so, allowing the black strands of her hair to frame her heart-shaped face. Her blue eyes practically glistened with satisfaction. "It's about damned time you realized that. Hold on. I think I won the pool. I'll have to check my ticket. Let's face it, that man has done everything short of renting a private plane and flying you to Paris to get you to see the light."

Cynthia set her reading glasses on one of the numerous files on her desk before standing and walking her way around so that she joined Laurel in one of the two guest chairs.

"Laurel, it's clear that he loves you for who *you* are. He took you home to his family, he's practically moved you into his apartment, and it's evident that he sees you as an equal in business and life. Only you see yourself on another level that technically doesn't really even exist. So my advice?" Cynthia reached over the arm of the chair to pat Laurel's knee. "Don't throw away what he's offering you because of self-doubt. You've come too far to cheat yourself out of every young girl's fantasy. You can have it all, Laurel. That is, if you can work it out to get out of your own damned way."

Laurel didn't get to respond. A small commotion came down

the hallway, with fellow employees leaving their offices to see what was taking place. She and Cynthia shared a look of concern before joining the others in the corridor, but it was the significant police presence in the large foyer that held everyone's attention.

Laurel immediately sought out Smith, who was coming out of the conference room behind Paul and Catherine. His gaze searched the crowd, displaying relief when he found her.

"What's going on here?" Paul asked, most likely having been summoned by Marilyn. The older woman was standing behind her desk with her fingers pressed to her lips in shock. "Detective Nielsen, I asked a question."

"Where is Grace Dorrance?"

"I'm sure she's in her—"

"I'm right here." Grace came around the corner of the trading room, a look of skepticism and fear written across her pale features. "What happened?"

"Grace Dorrance, you're under arrest for the murder of Brad Manon." Detective Nielson nodded toward one of the two officers who'd accompanied him into the building. "You have the right to remain..."

"I'll go call Rye Marshall," Cynthia muttered, shaking her head in disbelief. "It's all his fault that she's in this predicament to begin with."

That was most likely true, but Detective Nielsen didn't seem the type of officer to arrest someone without evidence.

What had the police found to link Grace to Brad?

Laurel closed the distance to Smith as she watched on in horror as the officer turned Grace around so that he could put her in handcuffs. This somehow seemed even more surreal than walking into Brad's office and finding him with his throat slashed.

"Smith, we have to do something." Laurel understood that Meg couldn't represent the entire office, but Josh had been given someone just as reputable. "I can't believe this is happening. I need to go with her."

"Good luck with that," Catherine Greenlee stated in a tone that was feigned sympathy. She even straightened her shoulders as if her comment gave her strength. "It seems I'm pulling my money out at just the right time, now, doesn't it? I'm sure Smith will have a better handle on his collection of employees when he opens his firm."

Laurel wanted to get into the woman's surgically enhanced face and tell her to shove her precious money up her own ass, but Smith's hand resting on her lower back prevented her from stooping to that level.

Somehow, in this very moment, everything became crystal clear.

Money *wasn't* the root of all evil.

People had a choice on whether to live their lives with good intentions. Manon Investments had a lot of clients who used their wealth for the good of humanity around the world— Gareth Nicollet being just one of them. She'd even heard Smith on the phone arranging various donations to some of the community centers around the city, though he requested his contributions remain anonymous. He wasn't seeking attention for himself, but rather doing his part to build a better community—her community.

"What's the saying?" Laurel murmured to Smith, who already had his car keys in hand. He was going to go with her to the police station. That small gesture caused her to believe that everything was going to be okay. First, there was something she needed to take care of before leaving the building. She was going to hell, anyway. She might as well enjoy the trip. "It's better to beg for forgiveness than ask for permission."

Catherine was still watching Grace being led away in handcuffs and escorted into the elevator when Laurel stood in front of the woman so that nothing she said could be misunderstood.

It was common knowledge that Manon Investments couldn't survive without Brad Manon to run the ship. Hedge funds were only as good as the portfolio manager. Normally, there would be a no-compete clause for anyone who chose to leave a firm such as this one, but that directive was no longer in play under the circumstances.

Catherine Greenlee no doubt assumed that she had a home for the money she'd placed into Manon Investments.

Well, that was no longer the case.

"Catherine, I don't believe Gallo Capital Management will be the right fit for you." Laurel genuinely smiled at the woman's confusion. Catherine even glanced toward Smith, as if to say he should do something about his lover. "I suggest taking your money and investing it into some etiquette classes or maybe a charm school, seeing as there are just some things money can't buy."

Smith mouth tilted at the corner, having understood exactly what Laurel had been referring to about forgiveness. After all, she'd just cost his new firm around four hundred million dollars.

"It seems as if you'll have to look elsewhere for your investments, Catherine. Now, if you'll excuse us, a friend of ours is in need."

Laurel would have relished having Smith escort her through the glass doors and toward the elevator, but her purse was still in her office. She didn't look back to see if Catherine was trying to speak with Paul or if she'd stormed out of the foyer in anger. The woman was no longer a blip on Laurel's radar. Out of sight, out of mind.

"You are hell on fashionable heels, my little minx." Smith pulled her into his arms the moment they were in private, kissing her passionately. After a minute, he finally allowed both of them to come up for air. "Does this mean you're going to be a part of Gallo Capital Management?"

"Yes," Laurel answered, a weight coming off her shoulders. It was freeing to finally shed all the doubts and insecurities that had plagued her for so long. "Yes, I'll take the position. Yes, I want to be an initial shareholder. Yes, I love you, Smith Gallo. And not necessarily in that order."

Laurel laughed when Smith wrapped his arms around her waist, lifting her high heels off the ground. The prospects for their future were endless, and the exhilaration made her want to call it a day and head back to his place. She would have loved to curl up in his bed, spending the afternoon reveling in what should have been a celebratory moment.

"Grace will be fine," Smith assured when her laughter faded and reality began to intrude. "Grab your purse, and we'll head down to the station. I'll give Meg a call to see if she can recommend a criminal attorney who can handle something of this magnitude."

She couldn't imagine what Grace was going through at the moment. Brad's murder had touched everyone in some way or other, but this arrest made it more than personal. Someone close to Laurel was about to have her life turned upside down. That was unacceptable.

"Smith?" Laurel stopped him from turning toward the door after he'd collected her purse. "Grace isn't a murderer. She isn't. We need to find out who killed Brad before Grace is blamed for a murder she didn't commit."

"We'll talk about this on the way to the station."

Smith had already pulled out his phone and would have

placed a call if Laurel hadn't taken the device from his hands. There was one more loose end she needed to tie up.

"Once we get things settled with Grace, I'd like to make a stop before we go home." Smith gave Laurel an inquisitive look. He was most likely expecting her request to have something to do with Grace, but this was a matter close to her heart and long overdue. "It's time for you to meet my mother, Harvard boy."

~ THE END ~

Thank you so much for reading the first book in the Office Roulette series! Grace and Rye's story continues in Motive, and you won't want to miss the next installment of this trilogy…

http://www.kennedylayne.com/motive.html

The Office Roulette trilogy continues with an epic battle between blame and forgiveness…

Rye Marshall had it all—wealth, prominence, and the love of his life. But nothing lasts forever, and his perfect world came crashing down around him. When the dust settled, he found himself alone and starting from a clean slate.

Grace Dorrance had made many mistakes in her life, but one stood out above the rest—an epic ending to a complex and passionate relationship. She left her former lover's life in complete ruins and tried her best never to look back at the wreckage.

Seconds chances are hard to come by, but even more difficult when Grace is arrested for a murder she didn't commit. This gives Rye the perfect motive to forgive and forget, allowing for new beginnings. Unfortunately, someone's playing a game of office roulette with everyone's lives.

Books by Kennedy Layne

Office Roulette Series
Means (Office Roulette, Book One)
Motive (Office Roulette, Book Two)
Opportunity (Office Roulette, Book Three)

Keys to Love Series
Unlocking Fear (Keys to Love, Book One)
Unlocking Secrets (Keys to Love, Book Two)
Unlocking Lies (Keys to Love, Book Three)
Unlocking Shadows (Keys to Love, Book Four)
Unlocking Darkness (Keys to Love, Book Five)

Surviving Ashes Series
Essential Beginnings (Surviving Ashes, Book One)
Hidden Ashes (Surviving Ashes, Book Two)
Buried Flames (Surviving Ashes, Book Three)
Endless Flames (Surviving Ashes, Book Four)
Rising Flames (Surviving Ashes, Book Five)

CSA Case Files Series
Captured Innocence (CSA Case Files 1)
Sinful Resurrection (CSA Case Files 2)
Renewed Faith (CSA Case Files 3)
Campaign of Desire (CSA Case Files 4)
Internal Temptation (CSA Case Files 5)
Radiant Surrender (CSA Case Files 6)
Redeem My Heart (CSA Case Files 7)

Red Starr Series

Starr's Awakening(Red Starr, Book One)
Hearths of Fire (Red Starr, Book Two)
Targets Entangled (Red Starr, Book Three)
Igniting Passion (Red Starr, Book Four)
Untold Devotion (Red Starr, Book Five)
Fulfilling Promises (Red Starr, Book Six)
Fated Identity (Red Starr, Book Seven)
Red's Salvation (Red Starr, Book Eight)

The Safeguard Series

Brutal Obsession (The Safeguard Series, Book One)
Faithful Addiction (The Safeguard Series, Book Two)
Distant Illusions (The Safeguard Series, Book Three)
Casual Impressions (The Safeguard Series, Book Four)
Honest Intentions (The Safeguard Series, Book Five)
Deadly Premonitions (The Safeguard Series, Book Six)

About the Author

First and foremost, I love life. I love that I'm a wife, mother, daughter, sister… and a writer.

I am one of the lucky women in this world who gets to do what makes them happy. As long as I have a cup of coffee (maybe two or three) and my laptop, the stories evolve themselves and I try to do them justice. I draw my inspiration from a retired Marine Master Sergeant that swept me off of my feet and has drawn me into a world that fulfills all of my deepest and darkest desires. Erotic romance, military men, intrigue, with a little bit of kinky chili pepper (his recipe), fill my head and there is nothing more satisfying than making the hero and heroine fulfill their destinies.

Thank you for having joined me on their journeys…

Email:

kennedylayneauthor@gmail.com

Facebook:

facebook.com/kennedy.layne.94

Twitter:

twitter.com/KennedyL_Author

Website:

www.kennedylayne.com

Newsletter:

www.kennedylayne.com/newslettertext.html